TROUBLE SHOOTER

TROUBLE SHOOTER

JACKSON COLE

THORNDIKE
CHIVERS

This Large Print edition is published by Thorndike Press®, Waterville, Maine USA and by BBC Audiobooks Ltd, Bath, England.

Published in 2005 in the U.S. by arrangement with Golden West Literary Agency.

Published in 2006 in the U.K. by arrangement with Golden West Literary Agency.

U.S. Hardcover 0-7862-7963-X (Western)
U.K. Hardcover 1-4056-3581-9 (Chivers Large Print)
U.K. Softcover 1-4056-3582-7 (Camden Large Print)

The text of this Large Print edition is unabridged.
Other aspects of the book may vary from the original edition.

Set in 16 pt. Plantin by Ramona Watson.

Printed in the United States on permanent paper.

═══

British Library Cataloguing-in-Publication Data available

═══

Library of Congress Cataloging-in-Publication Data

Cole, Jackson.
    Trouble shooter / by Jackson Cole.
       p. cm. — (Thorndike Press large print westerns)
    ISBN 0-7862-7963-X (lg. print : hc : alk. paper)
    1. Texas Rangers — Fiction.   2. Texas — Fiction.
    3. Large type books.   I. Title.   II. Thorndike Press large print Western series.
    PS3505.O2685T76 2005
    813'.54—dc22   2005015298

TROUBLE SHOOTER

CHAPTER 1

A crowd milled around the railroad station of Cameron, a crowd of brawny, clear-eyed men wearing rough corduroys, red, blue or plaid shirts and high-laced boots, the soles of which were liberally studded with hobnails or sharp spikes. Their hands bore the calluses of ax, saw and peavy handle and they had a rugged outdoor look to them. They jostled together, talked in boisterous tones and swore with vigor. An air of suppressed excitement prevailed.

Standing a little to one side was a giant of a man with heavy shoulders and abnormally long arms that hung loosely by his sides. His big-featured, handsome face wore a malicious smile as he glanced from time to time toward the far end of the platform, where a slim, nervous young man in store clothes stood. His thin face was tense, and slightly apprehensive. He kept opening and closing his fingers as he leaned forward to peer along the twin ribbons of steel stretching into the east until the parallel rails seemed to draw together and become one.

7

The terrain into which the railroad vanished was forbidding, an arid and profitless desert shimmering under the blazing Texas sun. A few miles west of the station, the desert was cut by a range of bleak hills that started up abruptly and raked the sky with their jagged crags. In line with the railroad there appeared to be a defile or pass slashing their granite breasts.

To the northeast were more hills that were, in contrast, low and heavily timbered. To the northwest was rolling rangeland gleaming green and amethyst to the skyline.

Others beside the young man kept peering eastward. The dwindling steel of the railroad apparently held a fascination for the group crowding the platform. Suddenly a voice rang out above the babble of talk, "Here she comes, boys! Get set!"

Against the brassy blue of the eastern sky appeared a pluming smudge of black. It shot straight upward in spasmodic spurts, spread and mushroomed in the wind, and rolled toward the cattle town. Under the smoke cloud appeared a dark object that swiftly grew in size. The rails began to sing and a low murmur became apparent as the crowd suddenly hushed.

The murmur grew to a mutter, a

grumble, a crackling roar that was the pounding exhaust of a locomotive speeding a heavy load. A long train of freight cars headed by several battered passenger coaches came thundering toward the town.

Up to the station boomed the train, and jolted to a stop. The doors of the coaches swung open and out poured a stream of men bearing turkeys, blanket rolls and bulging carpet bags. They were mostly of slighter build and younger than the big lumberjacks who thronged the platform, but a glance showed them to be the same. They hustled down the steps, chattering gaily among themselves.

With a bellow the loggers on the platform rushed forward. In split seconds a most amazing shindig was in progress. Fists were flying, and hobnailed boots. Men slugged, kicked, wrestled and swore appalling oaths. The whole length of the platform was a whirling, ducking, lunging mass of tangled humanity as more and more men poured from the coaches to reinforce their battling companions. The newcomers, though taken by surprise and outnumbered, were giving a good account of themselves.

"Shove the hellions back in the cars!" bellowed the loggers.

"Try and do it!" bawled the hellions.

The confusion was at its height when a final solitary figure sauntered out of the foremost coach and descended to the platform with leisurely steps, his lean, deeply bronzed face touched with a look of amused interest. He was a very tall man, much more than six feet, wide of shoulder, deep of chest, and lean of waist and hips. He wore the homely and efficient garb of the rangeland — faded blue overalls and shirt, vivid neckerchief looped about his sinewy throat, high-heeled boots of softly tanned leather, broad-brimmed "J.B." Encircling his waist were double cartridge belts and from the carefully worked and oiled cut-out holsters, thrust the plain black butts of heavy guns.

At the edge of the platform, Jim Hatfield paused and watched the proceedings with his black-lashed green eyes. The fight didn't look very serious to him. Black eyes and bloody noses would very likely be the extent of the casualties, and he felt no call to interfere, but he was curious to know what had started it.

Two big lumberjacks of the attacking force suddenly spotted him and, too excited for their eyes to properly register appearances, rushed toward him with a

10

bellow of profanity, fists swinging.

Hatfield did not move. He calmly appraised the attacking pair as they bounded forward. But as the loggers came within reach, he seemed to hit out with both hands at once.

The forward rush of the lumberjacks changed its course and ended with the crash of their big bodies on the boards. One stayed right where he was, arms flung wide. The other, spewing curses through the blood that streamed from his cut lips, scrambled to his feet and rushed again, his shaggy head bent low.

As the battering ram of flesh and bone lunged at him, Jim Hatfield weaved gracefully aside. His right hand, the fingers extended, chopped downward. The edge of his palm caught the charging logger on the side of his corded neck and seemed to literally drive him into the floor boards, where he stayed, writhing and groaning in agony.

The giant on the far side of the platform, who had been watching the riot with evident satisfaction, observed the downfall of the two loggers. The smile of cynical amusement vanished and his face flushed to a dark red. But even as he took a stride forward, huge hands knotted into fists, a

11

crashing report shattered the air. Double charges of buckshot screeched over the heads of the battlers, so close they felt the wind of their passing.

Standing in the road that edged the platform was a lanky old man holding a smoking shotgun. A big nickel badge gleamed on the front of his sagging vest. He flipped open the breech of the scattergun, ejected the spent shells, shoved in fresh cartridges and clanged the breech shut. His voice rang out. "The next two loads of blue whistlers go right through the middle of you horned toads! Bust it up if you want to keep airholes out of your hides!"

He turned to face the wrathful giant, who had whirled toward him, and swung the twin barrels of the shotgun to line with the other's middle.

"Radcliff," he said, "get your tree knockers out of here and head for your camp. I've had enough of this darn foolishness."

The big man glowered, and shook his fist at the sheriff. "Some day you'll go too far, McGregor," he rumbled. "I know my rights and I aim to protect 'em."

"You'll get all the protection coming to you under the law, but don't try taking the law into your own hands if you want to stay healthy," the sheriff returned coldly. "Get going, I said!"

The other hesitated, but the hammers of the shotgun abruptly clicked back to full cock. The sheriff's frosty eyes gleamed back of the black muzzles, his fingers tightened on the triggers. Radcliff swore under his breath, shot a venomous glance at Hatfield and strode across to where his men were bunched together, muttering and cursing.

"All right, boys," he said. "Get out of here. We'll finish this business later."

With menacing scowls over their shoulders, the battered lumberjacks obeyed. The equally battered newcomers shouted taunts and jeers after them.

Hatfield noticed that Radcliff did not accompany his hands. He stepped into the station.

The sheriff whirled on the whooping newcomers. "And that'll be enough out of you!" he bellowed. "Wallace, you get your bunch out of here, too. Why the devil did you have to squat in this section? Everything was peaceful till you showed up!"

"I know my rights, too, Sheriff, and I don't take the law in my own hands," replied the slightly built young man in store clothes, who was wiping blood from his bruised face.

The sheriff snorted something profane and walked around the corner of the building, from where he could keep an eye on the departing loggers. The young man strode over to Hatfield, holding out his hand.

"I saw what you did to those two bullies and I want to congratulate you," he said. "Their attack on you was unwarranted and without provocation. My name's Wallace, Clark Wallace."

Hatfield introduced himself and they shook hands. Wallace's clasp was firm and warm.

"It was a nice little reception committee, all right," Hatfield said. "Do they always welcome gents into this section that way?"

The other's battered features relaxed in a grin. "Not always," he replied. "Radcliff knew I was bringing in workers today, workers he had hoped to get, and either acted from pure cussedness or perhaps figured he could scare them off. Doesn't matter which. By the way, my logging is five miles up the Coronado Trail. If you are aiming to stay around here a while, I'd be very pleased to have you drop in on me. I'd like a talk with you. Well, I'll have to be getting my men to camp. Hope I'll see you soon."

"You may," Hatfield replied.

Wallace hurried off to where his men were waiting across the road. He had hardly gone when the big man, Radcliff, stepped from the station and approached Hatfield, a scowl on his face. Tall as he was, he had to raise his eyes a trifle to meet the level gaze of the man a stern old Lieutenant of Rangers named the Lone Wolf.

"So," he said in his rumbling voice, "so the little skunk is bringing in professional gun slingers to do his dirty work for him, eh? Well, it won't work. I've handled your kind before. I'll be seeing you."

"Look close the first time, you might not get a chance to look twice," Hatfield answered quietly.

Radcliff's fists knotted and he seemed about to explode, but the sheriff suddenly reappeared around the corner and jammed the muzzles of his shotgun into his belly.

"I said get going, Radcliff, and that's just what I mean," he said. "I don't give a darn if you are the big skookum he-wolf in this section, you can't run a whizzer over me, and you know it. Careful! This thing's got hair triggers!"

Radcliff ground his teeth, whirled and

15

strode up the platform. The sheriff uncocked his shotgun and tucked it under his arm. He gave Hatfield a hard look.

"Two-gun man, eh?" he remarked. "And what the devil do you want hereabouts?"

Hatfield smiled down at him from his great height, a dancing light in his green eyes. He liked this crusty old peace officer.

"Well, first off a surrounding of chuck wouldn't go bad," he replied as he fished out the makin's and deftly rolled a cigarette with the slim fingers of his left hand.

The sheriff bristled at the unexpected answer, but as Hatfield continued to smile, his even teeth flashing white against his bronzed face, he chuckled roughly.

"Reckon the question was sort of out of turn," he admitted, "but I've had so much trouble on my hands lately, I'm sort of beside myself. Every time I see a new face I expect something else to bust loose."

"Heard a feller might be able to tie onto a job of riding in this section," Hatfield said.

"Reckon that's so," the sheriff admitted. "What with the infernal logging operations and the darned railroads building through here, the cow business is booming and good hands are hard to come by. Reckon you can sign on with most any outfit up to the north except Bull Radcliff's Lazy B, the biggest in the section. I've a notion Bull don't feel very kind towards you after what you did to his logging foreman and that other jigger. I figure Chuck Hooley, he's the foreman, won't be able to turn his head for a week. You darn near broke his neck with that chop you gave him with the side of your hand. Chuck sets up to be a salty hombre and considerable of a fighter, but you sure took him down a peg today. Lucky for you, though, I happened along with my scattergun when I did. Bull was heading for you and Bull Radcliff is something to buck up against. You wouldn't have found him so easy to down. I've knowed Bull to be larruped by a single-tree and then beat the tar out of the feller who hit him."

"Uh-huh, reckon I was lucky," was Hatfield's smiling reply.

The sheriff measured him with a calculating eye. "Maybe," he agreed, "but then again maybe it was Bull who was lucky. I reckon you'll get a chance to find out if you stick around. Bull will be seeing you. Go slow about reaching for those guns if you tie up with him. Bull is chain lightning on the draw, and he don't calc'late to miss when he pulls the trigger."

"I just wear mine for ornaments," Hatfield replied without the trace of a smile.

"Uh-huh, I figured that when I noticed the way they're slung," the sheriff answered sarcastically. His voice took on a sterner note.

"I don't stand for folks taking the law in their own hands hereabouts if I can prevent it," he warned. "There's been enough of that already of late and I'm about fed up. So watch your step, cowboy. And incidentally, keep your eyes skun for Chuck Hooley. He's vicious as a sidewinder and never forgets. He's got a killing or two to his credit, that's pretty nigh to certain, though nobody was ever able to prove 'em on him. He won't forgive you that chop on the neck and he'll be out to even up the score; and he won't be a darn bit particular how he does it, just so long as he figures he can get away with it."

Hatfield nodded, glancing down the platform as the engine whistled two short blasts. The train, its westward run completed, was ready to pull into the yards.

"Got my horse in that car," Hatfield observed, nodding toward the cut-out. "Want to see about getting him unloaded."

"Speak to the agent," the sheriff advised. He lingered curiously as Hatfield made his request. The agent gave an order to a ordinate. The door of the car was rolleᴅ back and an unloading plank shoved into place. Hatfield walked up it and entered the car. A few minutes later he reappeared. The sheriff gave a low whistle as his eyes rested on the magnificent golden sorrel Hatfield led down the platform.

"That's the kind of a cayuse you dream about but never expect to see," the sheriff remarked.

"Uh-huh, old Goldy's quite a horse," Hatfield agreed, rubbing the glossy neck over which rippled a glorious black mane.

The sheriff stepped forward and extended a hand.

"Careful!" Hatfield warned as the sorrel's velvety lips raised up to expose milk-white teeth.

"It's all right, feller," Hatfield told him, "the sheriff's a good Injun."

"Darned if I don't believe he understood exactly what you said!" exploded Sheriff McGregor as Goldy dropped his lips over his teeth and craned his neck toward the reaching hand.

"He did," Hatfield replied briefly. "You've got a stand-in with him now. He doesn't go for strangers till I put my okay on them."

ld glanced over the sprawling web
ks across from the station, on many
ich stood freight and material cars,
busy switch engines shunted other
cars back and forth.

"A big yard," he commented.

"Uh-huh, it's the C & P assembling
yard," said the sheriff. "They aim to make
this a division point. The town's going to
boom. Is already booming for that matter.
A mile to the north the T & W is also
building west. Right now they're both
working hell-for-leather to bridge the
Alamita Gorge, five miles to the west of
here, and it's one hard chore. The first line
to reach Alpine Pass, thirty miles on to the
west, will control the trackage through that
coyote hole, there isn't room enough for
two lines, and the other will have to lease
from the winner of the race. Big mail and
express contracts at stake, too. Reckon it's
worth millions to the winner. This division
of the C & P is being financed by local
capital. Otherwise it wouldn't be built and
they'd take the northern route. Lots of
fellers in this section got just about all they
own tied up in the project. There's been
trouble and likely to be more. Bull Radcliff
opposed the coming of the road through
here and made a lot of enemies. He got so

mad about it, blaming the C & P for everything, that when the T & W mighty un-
expectedly started building this way, too,
he agreed to supply them with wood for
ties and bridge timbers."

"I see," Hatfield nodded thoughtfully.
"And that's where the logging business
comes in, eh?"

"That's right," replied the sheriff, "and
the darned logging business is the center of
all the trouble hereabouts. Bull has been in
the logging business, in a way, for a long
time. He owns a fine stand of pine over
east and has a sawmill and for years sawed
up boards and stuff for building. Up to the
north he owned another big stand, of live
oak. Live oak ain't much good for building
purposes and Bull never thought much of
the holding. So when that darned young
Wallace came along and wanted to buy the
stand, Bull sold it to him, cheap. Wallace
must have known something. Not so long
after he bought from Bull, along comes the
news that the railroad was coming through
here. Live oak is just about tops for
crossties and bridge timbers, so Wallace
contracts with the C & P to provide all
they would need, which is plenty. When
Bull heard about it he swore he'd been
flim-flammed, and he hates Wallace's guts.

He hasn't any live oak, but he's got plenty of burr oak, which is almost but not quite as good."

"And there's been trouble between them?"

"Uh-huh, they both been having trouble. A month or so back Wallace had his storehouse burned to the ground. A week later somebody set fire to Bull's sawmill. Watchman found the blaze just in time. Somebody took a shot at Wallace, knocked a hunk of meat off his shoulder. Bull swears he's been shot at twice. Each blames the other for what's happened. Nice mess!"

"Decidedly," Hatfield agreed. "And what started the row today?"

"They both need more hands," the sheriff explained. "Bull learned a logging project over to the east in Uvalde county was folding up business. He figured he'd hire the hands they were letting go. But somehow Wallace beat him to it and hired them first. Bull swore he'd run 'em back to Uvalde. Plum loco notion, but I reckon that was what he was trying to do today. I heard about it and got here with my scattergun a mite late. The devil knows where it'll all end. Come on over to the Greasy Sack, about the best saloon in town, and I'll buy a drink. Been nice talking to you. Sort of got things off my chest."

"I need a place to put up my horse and a room for myself," Hatfield said.

"Hitch him to the rack in front of the saloon and after we wash the dust out I'll show you a livery stable," the sheriff replied.

Hatfield agreed and they entered the Greasy Sack together.

CHAPTER 2

The saloon was a big one and well appointed. Although it was early evening, there was already a considerable crowd at the bar and scattered about the room, mostly cowhands, who were loudly discussing the row on the station platform. Sheriff McGregor nodded cordially to a man standing near the end of the bar.

"Howdy, Lee," he greeted, "how's things going up to the road-building?"

"About as well as could be expected under present conditions," the other replied in a quiet voice. "I see Clark Wallace brought in another lot of trouble makers."

"Reckon they won't make much trouble if they're let alone," grunted McGregor. "Wallace hires 'em to get out crossties and timbers, not to start rukuses."

"Hope you're right," replied Lee in tones that showed he was plainly unconvinced. He glanced questioningly at Hatfield.

"Hatfield, I want you to know Alton Lee," introduced the sheriff. "Lee has the contract for putting the T & W line through this section."

Lee shook hands with a firm grip. There was an inscrutable look in his deeply blue and very clear eyes as they took in the Ranger from head to foot. He was a slender man about six feet tall. He had a firm mouth, a prominent chin and his features were cameo-like in their regularity. His hair was crisply golden and inclined to curl. He was dressed in black relieved only by the snow of his ruffled shirt front. There was a steely look about him and his slenderness, Hatfield felt, was the slenderness of a finely tempered rapier blade. His face was pleasant enough when he smiled, otherwise expressionless.

"The sort of jigger who doesn't give out much of himself," the Lone Wolf thought. "Looks to be a regular hombre, though."

Lee finished his drink and placed his empty glass on the bar.

"I must go," he said. "Got a number of things to attend to, but I'll be back later. Tomorrow is payday and some of my hellions will be down here before long, and they sometimes need a bit of looking after. Glad to have met you, Hatfield. Take care of yourself, McGregor."

Sheriff McGregor watched the construction man pass through the swinging doors, walking with the lithe grace that bespeaks perfect muscular coordination.

"I like that feller," he said, "but I'm darned if I can make him out. I've a notion he's hard as nails for all his quiet way of speaking. He's got as tough an outfit working for him up there on the grade as I ever laid eyes on, but I've noticed that when Lee gives an order those hellions jump. Got a lot of responsibility on his hands. The T & W looks to him to beat the C & P in the construction race. Reckon if anybody can do it he can. He sure knows his business, and I understand he's a tophand engineer."

Hatfield was interested. He himself had graduated from a famous school of engineering, but shortly afterward his father had been murdered by wideloopers and he joined the Rangers in order to run down the killers.

"Looks capable, all right," he agreed. "Where'd he come from?"

"Pennsylvania, I believe," replied the sheriff. "Made his reputation building railroad over there, I heard. Wouldn't be surprised if he owns a considerable interest in the T & W. Anyhow, he packs influence. I was over by the bridge building a while back, when they were just laying the approaches. There was a private car there with the president of the road and a lot of other big bugs. Some sort of a discussion as to methods started and the president thought something should be done a certain way. Then all of a sudden Lee spoke up. 'No, that's not practical,' he said. 'I've already decided how the matter is to be handled.' And that was that. Nobody argued with him. No, I don't know a great deal about him. Doesn't talk much about himself. Doesn't talk much at all, for that matter. Well, if you're ready, I'll show you that stable. Feller has good clean rooms upstairs over the stalls if you like to sleep close to your horse."

To reach the stable they followed a quiet side street and then threaded their way through a narrow lane formed by pyramidical stacks of steel rails on one side and the blank wall of a long warehouse on the other. There was barely room for Goldy to pass.

"Don't jostle 'em, feller," Hatfield warned. "You might start one of those heaps rolling down and squash us."

"C & P material yard," said the sheriff, jerking his thumb toward the rails. "This is a short cut to the stable. Otherwise we'd have to go clean around the yard."

Suitable quarters for Goldy were obtained without difficulty and Hatfield secured a comfortable room over the stalls.

"Here's a key to the outer door," said the stablekeeper. "Don't usually give 'em out, but anybody the sheriff brings around can have one. You won't have to wake me up to get in if you come around late. Reckon you'll be getting all set for payday tomorrow, eh, Sheriff? Big times!"

"Uh-huh, for some folks, but just a prime headache for me," grunted McGregor.

The sheriff headed for his office and Hatfield returned to the Greasy Sack for something to eat.

He found the big saloon filling up. In addition to the cowhands lining the bar and wrangling over cards at the tables, there was an increasing crowd of construction workers and other hands from the railroads. None of the loggers were present at the moment.

"The sort of gathering you can expect most anything from," the Lone Wolf mused as he ate an excellent meal. "I've a notion this is a lively hangout later in the evening. See they've got an orchestra and a dance floor. Three roulette wheels and a faro bank, too, and those dealers look like they know what it's all about. Uh-huh, not a bad pueblo, this Cameron. Got a notion Captain Bill was right. I'll enjoy coiling my twine here for a spell."

Hatfield noticed that the railroad workers kept to themselves in a compact group. A little later another bunch of like characters entered the saloon and ranged themselves at the far end of the bar. Hatfield quickly deduced the first group represented the C & P construction hands, the other the T & W. It was obvious from the compressed lips, the lowering brows and the menacing glances exchanged from time to time that little love was lost between the two outfits. This was not remarkable. Hatfield knew that such men took their work seriously and had an intense loyalty to the outfit that employed them. The race to Alpine Pass was in the nature of a knock-down and drag-out fight where they were concerned.

"And when that redeye they're pouring down gets to working there's liable to be fireworks," he predicted. "I've a notion Sheriff McGregor is likely to be a busy man before the night's over."

The saloon continued to fill up. The musicians arrived, tuned their instruments and struck up a lively number. Girls in short spangled skirts and extremely low-cut bodices appeared. The thump of boots and the sprightly click of high heels resounded. The crowd steadily grew more boisterous as more and more of the construction workers from the railroads filed in. Remarks began to be tossed back and forth between the two outfits.

Abruptly the explosion came. The T & W outfit, Hatfield noticed, was the more aggressive, but it was a scornful epithet from a C & P hand that opened the ball. A big tracklayer came bounding across the room, fists doubled, face working with anger. Behind him streamed his fellows, ready to back up anything he might do. The C & P hands braced themselves grimly against the onslaught.

But before the two factions could close, there was an unexpected interruption. A slender figure in black streaked through the swinging doors and between the groups. His outstretched palm, backed by an arm as rigid as a steel bar, caught the big trackman on the chest and hurled him back.

"Get back to the bar and stop this nonsense," Alton Lee said quietly, as quietly as if he were inviting the man to have a drink.

The tracklayer glared, his red hair bristling, his face flushing scarlet. "Darn you!

I've stood enough from you!" he bawled. Gathering himself together, he rushed at the smaller man. Behind him crowded his companions, for the moment bereft of reason in their anger.

Alton Lee did not waver. His hand flashed up, something spatted against his palm and slashed downward in a vicious, raking stroke.

There was a crunch of steel against flesh and bone and the big trackman thudded to the floor, blood pouring from his split scalp. His companions recoiled before the rock-steady twin black muzzles of a heavy calibre double-barreled derringer that yawned toward them.

"Pick up that clown and throw him out," Lee ordered in his quiet, conversational tones. "When he gets his senses back, tell him that if he shows up on the job day after tomorrow, I'll shoot him on sight. And that goes for any of the rest of you that don't show up the day after payday, no matter how drunk you get tomorrow. Understand?"

It was plain they understood. They shuffled back to their drinks, muttering together in low tones, but with all the fight taken out of them. Alton Lee, without a glance at the man whose skull he'd broken, turned and walked from the saloon.

CHAPTER 3

Hatfield had half risen from his seat when the shindig started. Now he sat gazing after Alton Lee's retreating form, the concentration furrow deep between his black brows, a sure sign the Lone Wolf was doing some hard thinking.

"That was the fastest and smartest handling of a sleeve gun I ever saw," he told himself. "The iron just happened in his hand. And he hit like the kick of a mule. If that jigger hasn't got a fractured skull he's lucky."

A beefy individual with a handlebar mustache and a worried look came bustling forward, two swampers trailing at his heels. He was, Hatfield rightly judged, the proprietor of the Greasy Sack. He ordered the swampers to pack the injured man into the back room and patch him up. Then he retired to the far end of the bar, shaking his head and grumbling under his mustache. His perturbation was not unwarranted, Hatfield felt.

"Like riding herd on a bunch of peevish

grizzlies," he chuckled. "Hello! Here comes what might be more trouble."

Lunging through the swinging doors were the massive shoulders of Bull Radcliff. Beside him was his logging foreman, Chuck Hooley, whose head was twisted around at a painful angle. Evidently he hadn't yet fully recovered from the chop on his neck.

If Radcliff had any notions of making trouble they were not put in action. His eyes roved over the room and came to rest on Jim Hatfield's face with a fierce and menacing twinkle. Hooley also glowered at the Ranger and muttered something to his boss. However, they lumbered to the bar, ordered drinks and stood talking in low tones, their heads close together. After downing a couple of slugs they left the place without as much as a glance in Hatfield's direction.

Hatfield thoughtfully rolled and smoked a cigarette. The crowd was still boisterous, but there was no more hurling of sarcastic remarks by the two railroad factions. The cowboys, who had enjoyed the row while it lasted, were chuckling together over their drinks. The games were busy and the dance floor crowded. Hatfield decided there was little likelihood of any more trouble breaking loose for the present. What happened evidently had a sobering effect on the railroad workers. They quite likely figured that Lee was not far off and keeping an eye on them.

Finishing his smoke, Hatfield pinched out the butt and left the saloon. He felt a little shut-eye was in order. He followed the dimly lit street to the lane between the stacked rails and the warehouse and turned into the narrow opening. As he threaded his way between the huge piles of steel that pyramided high above his head, a slight creaking sound caused him to glance upward. He leaped forward in a convulsive bound as with a clanging roar, an avalanche of the ponderous rails thundered down toward him. The end of one brushed his shoulder and hurled him violently to the ground. One spinning length of steel fanned his face with its lethal breath as it flew over his prostrate form. Another thudded to the ground beside him and showered him with dust and bits of earth.

Dizzy from shock, he scrambled to his feet, blinking the dust from his eyes. Then he darted around the end of the disrupted pile, sensed a flicker of movement amid the shadows and hurled himself sideways and down.

Lances of reddish flame gushed the darkness. There was a thunder double reports so closely spaced as almost one. Hatfield felt the wind of passing lead and heard its spiteful whine. Whipping his guns from their holsters he sent a stream of slugs raking back and forth where he had seen the flash of the drygulcher's gun. With his sixes still spouting flame he rolled sideways, then lay tense, his thumbs hooked over the cocked hammers. His ears rang from the roar of his own guns, but he thought he heard a swift patter of footsteps fading into the distance. He got to his feet and glided forward, cocked guns jutting out in front of him, every nerve strung tense. Nothing moved amid the shadows, there was no sound, no sign of another presence. He paused at the spot from whence the shots had come and strove to pierce the gloom.

There was a moon, but it was low in the sky and its wan beams fell only between the piles of rails. Close by was a silvery patch that shimmered on the tufts of grass. He saw something white and stooped to pick it up. His brows drew together as he turned the small short cylinder over between his fingers, staring at it intently. It was only the butt of a half-smoked cigarette, but he pped it into his pocket. He stood listening a moment longer, ejecting the spent shells from his guns and replacing them with fresh cartridges. Nothing happened and there was no sign of anybody coming to investigate the shooting. Doubtless shots were not uncommon enough in Cameron to arouse much curiosity. He began looking over the ground near the scattered rails.

Nearby he found a stout timber with a rope tied to one end, with which the drygulcher had doubtless levered the top rails to send them avalanching down the sloping side of the pyramided pile, taking others along with them. He had set the pry in place and then stood behind the pile and by pulling down hard on the rope was able to set the mass in motion when he heard or saw Hatfield pass beneath it.

"Powerful hellion, all right," Hatfield mused. "Those darn things weigh three thousand pounds, they're thirty-foot lengths, and an average man couldn't budge one, even with the leverage provided by that pry. An ingenious arrangement, too. He could stay down here out of sight and still tip over the top rails."

The knot which secured the rope to the beam was unusual and interested the

Ranger. "Not the kind of knot you're likely to see in cow country," he told himself. "What's known as a surgeon's knot.

"May not mean anything," he decided, "but then again it might mean a lot. And the cigarette butt. That may mean nothing also, but you never can tell. The two together might constitute one of the little slips the owlhoot brand always make, sooner or later. Something to think about, anyhow."

Holstering his guns he proceeded cautiously past the rail heaps till he reached the stable door. No one was in sight. He used the key the keeper gave him and entered the building quietly. Goldy snorted a welcome and craned his head to Hatfield's reaching hand.

Before going to bed, Hatfield cleaned and oiled his guns. "Looks like somebody hereabouts doesn't like me," he told the big Colts. "A smart jigger, all right — lots of wrinkles on his horns. Figured out I'd have to pass those piles of rails on the way to the stable and rigged up his contraption to tumble them down on me. If he hadn't made a little noise prying the top ones loose, I'd have been right underneath the heap. Then when they picked up what was left of me, it would have appeared to be nothing but an accident. A sidewinder with plenty of cold nerve, too. Hung around to make sure the rails got me and to mow me down if they didn't."

Holstering the guns and placing them ready to hand, he rolled a cigarette and smoked thoughtfully. Ominous possibilities were forming around what had appeared to be but a routine Ranger chore. He smiled grimly as he recalled Captain Bill McDowell's words when he gave him the assignment.

"Should be sort of a vacation for you, Jim," Captain Bill said. "Nothing to do but hang around and see that nothing busts loose. There's the making of trouble, of course, in that railroad building race to Alpine Pass, and I figured we'd better keep an eye on it. Don't have to worry much about the C & P. Old Jaggers Dunn, your friend, who runs it, is a square shooter and don't stand for no nonsense. But the crowd back of the T & W ain't over particular about what methods they use to get what they want. They usually manage to keep inside the law, but they sometimes skate mighty close to the outside edge. So if you see anything off-color building, bust it up."

Captain Bill hadn't counted on the logging feud, which Hatfield decided had the makings of plenty of trouble. However, he didn't appear particularly displeased at what looked to be a rather alarming prospect. He went to bed and slept soundly.

CHAPTER 4

It was not very late when Hatfield arose, but the main street of Cameron was already black with men, and more trains of flat cars were rolling in from the west, each disgorging a turbulent load of workers.

The construction workers were not the only ones in for the payday celebration. There were plenty of cowhands from the spreads up to the northwest, and loggers from both camps were in evidence. The saloons were doing a good business, although it was nothing to what was to come later in the day when the paycar arrived and began handing out the fortune in gold that would burn holes in the pockets of the workers till it was spent.

Shopkeepers stood in their open doorways, alert and expectant. Waxen-faced dealers in sober black sat behind stacks of chips at the gaming tables. Shirt-sleeved bartenders polished glasses behind the gleaming bars. Dance floor girls gathered in groups, chattering noisily, their bright eyes gleaming with anticipation. The lunch counters were crowded with men who thought it wise to line their bellies with chuck before getting down to the important business of drinking.

After a good breakfast at the Greasy Sack, Hatfield strolled to the railroad station, where the crowd was thickest, every eye turned to the east, from which direction the paycar would come.

Suddenly a shout went up that swelled to a roar. Far off to the east a black dot had appeared, crowned by a wavering plume of smoke.

"Here comes our money!" yelled a brawny tracklayer. "Line up, boys! Pa-a-ay dirt!"

The locomotive with its single coach was travelling fast. Very few minutes passed before the paycar boomed into town and came to a screeching halt on a spur beside the station.

Armed guards descended and took up their posts. The paycar doors opened, the brass grilled windows banged up and a steady stream of men began filing in one door and out the other. Payday at Cameron was a reality.

Among the crowd Hatfield saw Bull Radcliff talking earnestly with Alton Lee. Beside Radcliff was his logging foreman,

41

Chuck Hooley, who didn't appear to be taking part in the conversation. Hooley's face suddenly twisted in a scowl and Hatfield followed the direction of his gaze. Riding into town by way of the Coronado Trail, which was plainly in view from the station, was young Clark Wallace.

"Looks like all the boys are gathering," Hatfield mused, "and if they happen to get together there'll be trouble!"

By noon all the workers at the western camp had arrived in town. Hatfield was surprised to see another train booming across the prairie from the hills. He walked slowly toward the railroad and watched it approach. He heard the chuckle of the exhaust swell and deepen, the low rumble become a grinding roar. Abruptly the exhaust shut off, the couplers clanked together as the train quickly lost speed. The engine lurched around a final curve and rolled along the straight stretch of track that ran close to the walls of the new roundhouse. The switch to the lead that led to the yards flashed red, the engineer slackened the speed still more with a light application of the air brakes.

The slowing locomotive was in the shadow of the roundhouse wall, nosing its way to the switch. Hatfield could see the engineer leaning out of the cab, one hand on the automatic airbrake handle. The fireman stood in the gangway between the locomotive and the tender, gazing out over the town.

Without the slightest warning a cloud of yellow smoke gushed from under the locomotive. There was a deafening roar, a rending of metal and a rumble of cascading bricks. Through the turmoil knifed a scream of agony cut off short.

Through the billowing smoke cloud, Hatfield, half stunned by the shock of the explosion, saw the locomotive actually rise in the air. It careened off the tracks and turned over. An instant later there was another thundering roar as the boiler exploded. Huge chunks of steel whizzed through the air. A small building near the tracks was torn to pieces by a section of the hurtling boiler. More bricks flew wildly from the shattered roundhouse. A cloud of steam streaked through the smoke and for a moment all details of the catastrophe were blotted out.

The smoke and steam quickly dissolved into the air and Hatfield saw that there was a wide and deep crater where the tracks had been an instant before. One whole side of the roundhouse had been torn away.

The roof sagged crazily on its splintered beams. The turntable had been blown from its pivot and lay in the pit. Of the fireman and engineer nothing was to be seen.

The town was in a turmoil of near panic. Crowds ran from the saloons and eating places, shouting, yelling, gesticulating. Nobody knew at the moment what had happened. Soon, however, the scene of the disaster was packed with a milling throng that stared into the crater hollowed out by the explosion, bawled questions, swore luridly.

Jim Hatfield, his eyes as cold as windswept ice, shouldered his way to the front. A score of paces distant from the track he spotted a portion of the mangled body of the engineer. The fireman was apparently nothing but scattered fragments. Parts of the locomotive were strewn in every direction. Splintered crossties and twisted rails lay about.

Sheriff McGregor came burrowing through the crowd, with him a white-faced man that Hatfield later learned was the shop superintendent.

"Dynamite!" the sheriff was rumbling. "The hellions planted dynamite under the rails and set it off when the train came along."

"But it couldn't be," the superintendent was protesting. "The track is patrolled all the time, ever since that explosion in the cut over to the west. This section along here, and the yards, are watched every minute of the night and day. How could anybody have worked here long enough to plant dynamite?"

"There's the evidence before your eyes," the sheriff pointed out grimly.

Glancing about, he caught sight of Hatfield. "Did you see what happened?" he asked. "There was an explosion before the boiler let go, wasn't there?"

"There was," Hatfield replied. "It was dynamite, all right. Couldn't have been anything else. It let go under the engine. The boiler didn't cut loose until after the engine turned over and bared the crown sheet and then sent water sloshing over it again."

"What did I tell you?" the sheriff said to the super. "I worked too long in the mines not to know. Of all the infernal snake-blooded things to do!"

"Thank God that was a train carrying tools and equipment for repairs," said the superintendent, mopping the sweat from his ashen face. "It could have been one of those trains loaded with men!"

45

There was a swirl and eddy in the crowd. Hatfield saw the massive form of Bull Radcliff plowing through. With him were Chuck Hooley and Alton Lee.

Radcliff paused, once he had gotten through the throng, which opened for him when they saw who it was, and stared at the wreckage. He was about to speak when a slightly built young man strode forward and halted directly in front of him. It was Clark Wallace. His eyes were like two splinters of sapphire in his bronzed face.

His voice rang out, "A good chore, Radcliff! You should be proud of this one. The best ever! Blew two poor devils to bits! Yes, you sure ought to be proud of this one!"

Radcliff stared at him, his jaw dropping. He grew red, then pale, then flushed fiery red again. His mouth snapped shut like a bear trap on its kill.

"Why, blast you!" he roared. "Blast you, I'll . . ."

His huge fist shot forward. If it had landed, it would have smashed the younger man's face to a pulp.

But it didn't land. Even as it whizzed through the air, slender, bronzed fingers like rods of steel caught Radcliff's wrist, checked and diverted the blow with seemingly ridiculous ease and swung the lumberman around to face the man he already felt he had little cause to love. Hatfield's voice was quiet as he let go the other's wrist.

"He's nigh onto a hundred pounds under your weight. Cool down, Radcliff, your twine's dragging."

Radcliff's anger boomed to frantic rage. He gave a bellow and went for his gun. His hand gripped the butt of the big Colt sagging low on his right thigh, but before he could unleather it, those steely fingers again closed on his wrist. And this time Jim Hatfield wasn't fooling. Radcliff's bellow turned to a howl of pain as the terrible grip ground his wrist bones together. His hand opened spasmodically and released the gun butt. He swung his left fist in a crushing blow.

But once more his fist missed its mark. He was whirled around, his arm cramped behind his back and the intolerable leverage on his elbow and shoulder joints brought him rising on his tip-toes, his face convulsed with pain.

The whole thing had happened in seconds, paralyzing the onlookers for an instant, but as Hatfield held Radcliff raging and helpless, Chuck Hooley dropped his hand to his gun.

Hatfield, the full force of his icy eyes on the logging boss' face, spoke a single word, "Don't!"

Under the menace in those suddenly terrible eyes, Hooley stiffened and stayed right where he was.

Hatfield spoke again, his voice quiet, and full of the respect due an older man.

"I'm not on the prod against you, sir, no matter what you may think," he told Radcliff. "I'm just trying to keep you from doing something you'd be mighty ashamed of a minute later. Get your feet on the ground and act up to your standing in the community. Be good if I turn you loose?"

"Y— yes — darn you!" gasped Radcliff.

Hatfield released his arm. Radcliff turned around, rubbing his numbed wrist and glaring at the man who had worsted him. His anger seemed charged with utter bewilderment.

"I ain't going to be accused of something I didn't have anything to do with!" he roared, glaring at Clark Wallace.

Then Wallace did something that caused him to soar in Hatfield's estimation.

"I apologize, Radcliff," he said. "I had no call to say what I did, seeing as I have nothing on which to base it."

He turned and walked away, leaving

Radcliff staring after him dazedly. He shook his shaggy head and turned to Hatfield.

"Feller," he said thickly, "today you did something nobody else was ever able to do. I hate your guts and I aim to even up the score some time, but by God you're a man!"

He plunged off through the crowd, Chuck Hooley, with a vindictive glance at Hatfield, trailing after him.

CHAPTER 5

Hatfield had a feeling that eyes were upon him. So strong was the feeling that he glanced about, to meet the cynically amused gaze of Alton Lee. Apparently the engineer was not displeased at the discomfort suffered by the arrogant Radcliff.

"Well," remarked Sheriff McGregor, "I wouldn't have believed there was a man in Texas who could do it."

"Reckon I sort of caught him off balance," Hatfield replied with a smile.

"Uh-huh, it looked that way," the sheriff said dryly.

After the crowd dispersed and what could be picked up of the dead fireman and engineer was carried away, Hatfield and the sheriff examined the fragments of the wrecked locomotive and estimated the depth and size of the crater the dynamite had hollowed out.

Hatfield was particularly interested in the twisted rails and splintered crossties. Finally he found a ponderous oaken tie, or rather, half a one, some distance from the right-of-way.

"This is the one the sticks were under, all right," he told the sheriff. "Half of it plumb blown away and powder burns on the end here. But how was it done? Looks like they must have used some sort of timing device, but how did they set it to explode the charge right at the time that train was pulling over this particular spot? A dozen trains passed this way since morning, and it's sure for certain they didn't plant the stuff after daylight. The material train wasn't running on a schedule, and even if it had been, the timing would have had to be split-second. It's a puzzler, all right."

Again he went over the whole locality with the utmost care, until he had satisfied himself there were no hidden wires that led to an electric detonator concealed somewhere. No, the charge had not been fired from a distance. A timing apparatus of some kind appeared to be the only explanation. But that the timing had been, by pure coincidence, set for the exact moment the material train would pass over the spot seemed ridiculous.

"There's the remote possibility, of course," he said to the sheriff, "that the charge was fired by the shock of the passing train, but if this was so, why wasn't it exploded by one of the dozen trains that passed over the rails before the material train arrived? And that pretty well rules out the notion of a trembler, too."

"You sure sling some big words, and sling 'em plumb accurate for a wandering cowhand," the sheriff commented.

"Perhaps, for a wandering cowhand," Hatfield smilingly agreed.

"You and Alton Lee ought to get together for a gabfest," remarked McGregor. "You talk alike sometimes."

"Maybe we will," Hatfield predicted. He examined the shattered crosstie again.

"You say Clark Wallace cuts only live oak on his holding?" he asked.

"That's right," agreed the sheriff. "He ain't got nothing else. As I told you, Bull Radcliff cuts burr oak. That's all he's got excepting for his pine over to the east, since he sold his stand of live oak to Wallace. Why?"

"I was just wondering," Hatfield parried, and deftly changed the subject. He did not want the sheriff to know, at the moment, that the crosstie under which the dynamite had apparently been placed had been cut from a burr oak trunk. It might not mean a thing, but it was a bit of coincidence that puzzled the Lone Wolf.

McGregor eyed the wreckage gloomily. "Well, no matter how it was done, it ended in cold-blooded murder," he said. "Somebody had ought to stretch rope for it. I'm going to swear in a half dozen more special deputies. It won't make for better feeling between those two infernal railroad outfits, and I don't want a riot busting loose.

"I wish young Wallace hadn't gone shooting off his mouth like he did," he added in worried tones. "Radcliff has made enough enemies as it is, without a thing like that being blabbed around. And despite his bullheadedness and general cussedness, I just can't see Radcliff doing a thing like this. I wouldn't put it past Chuck Hooley, but I'd never have given him credit for brains enough to figure it out."

Hatfield was silent.

The tragedy had for the moment put a decided damper on the payday celebration. Men stood about in tense groups, talking in low tones, their exhilaration and pleasurable excitement of the morning dead as ditch water.

A gang was hastily gotten together to repair the disrupted tracks. The workers moved cautiously, handling their picks and shovels and bars in gingerly fashion, as if fearing unexploded dynamite sticks might be concealed in the debris.

The shattered roundhouse was cleared up a bit, the turntable replaced on its pivot. The broken wall would be rebuilt tomorrow and the sagging roof shored up.

Meanwhile, the tight groups had dissolved. Men stopped looking apprehensively over their shoulders. Music and laughter began to be heard again. After all, it was payday, and death, sudden and sharp, was too familiar a thing to the construction workers and the cowhands to create any very lasting impression. By the time the lovely blue dusk of twilight sifted down from the hills, Cameron was booming.

Hatfield decided something to eat was in order and repaired to the Greasy Sack to get it. While he was eating, Clark Wallace came in, spotted him and dropped into an empty chair at his table.

"I want to thank you for saving me from getting all my teeth knocked out," the young lumberman said. "If Radcliff's fist had landed I guess I'd still be trying to regain consciousness. I'd have had it coming, though," he admitted frankly. "I had no business saying what I did, when I couldn't prove it."

"But you believed it," Hatfield observed.

"I did, and I do," Wallace returned.

"Do you really believe Radcliff capable of cold-blooded murder?" Hatfield asked curiously.

"Perhaps not deliberately," Wallace replied. "But I consider him stupid enough in some ways not to realize what blowing up a train or the roundhouse might entail. Besides," he added significantly, "I've been shot at from ambush, and that could have very well constituted murder, if the fellow's aim had been a little better."

"And you hold Radcliff responsible?"

"Who else?" Wallace countered. "I haven't any other enemies that I know of. Why should anybody else want to kill me?"

Hatfield couldn't answer that one, yet.

"I've learned considerable about Radcliff since I came here," Wallace continued. "He used to be a pretty cold proposition. Got his start running wet cows across the Rio Grande and, I've heard, by way of smuggling, too. Oh, I know such things are looked on lightly in this section of the country, and many a respectable business man and ranch owner got started that way, but it does throw a light on Radcliff's background. No doubt but he's got some killings to his credit, though I won't say they weren't in fair fight. Trouble with him is that he ran things to suit himself for so many years that he can't tolerate any change or having his opinions disregarded."

Hatfield nodded thoughtfully. There was much truth in what Wallace said. He was familiar with the Bull Radcliff type, arrogant, intolerant barons of the open range, a law unto themselves, accustomed to being deferred to, impatient of any change in the accepted order of things that worked so well to their personal advantage. He could see Radcliff flying into a black rage when his neighbors of greater vision decided that the section needed better transportation facilities and, ignoring his dictates, banded together to bring in the railroad. Then the coming of the rival line, the T & W, provided him with opportunity for taking out his spite on the offenders.

Wallace glanced at the clock over the bar. "Got to be going," he said. "My boys are drinking in a place farther down the street and I figure I'd better keep an eye on them. We've had enough trouble around here for one day. I hope you will ride up to my cutting soon. I would like to show you around the holding, and I want to talk to you about something."

"I'll try to make it tomorrow," Hatfield

promised. Wallace nodded and took his departure.

Hatfield finished his meal and rolled a cigarette. The table was in a corner, near the wall. He shoved his chair back, tilted it till the back rested against the wall and hooked his high heels over a rung. Where he sat he was in the shadow cast by a post supporting the ceiling, his features but a blur to anybody passing nearby. So it was not remarkable that Bull Radcliff and Alton Lee did not notice him when they took a table only a few feet distant. Hatfield's keen ears caught most of the conversation that passed between them.

"You'll have to do better, Radcliff," Lee was saying. "I can't use a large proportion of the stuff you're sending me. It's not properly grained and a lot of it's too small. It just won't do. And you're holding up the whole project by causing unnecessary delay in spanning the gorge. Until the bridge is up and steel laid across it we are practically at a standstill, and that darned C & P bunch are going great guns with the stuff Wallace delivers to them. I'm at my wit's end about this business. I'm trying to rush some suitable stuff from back east, but there are unavoidable delays there and I'm afraid it won't reach us soon enough to do any good. So it's up to you. You've got to do something about it, and quickly, too. You know how important it is to the road, and to me, that we don't lose out in the race to the Pass. There's a fortune at stake, and it's unbearable to think of losing it because of a few crossties and bridge timbers."

Radcliff swore a rumbling oath, his face darkened with anger. "Up there to the north is the stuff we need," he said. "Plenty of it, and easy to get at. That blasted Wallace! He's to blame for all this trouble, flim-flamming me out of that stand of live oak. I have to pick and cull, and sweat my brains out to get those infernal sticks. How was I to know that so much of that darn burr oak would be off-grain and rotten at heart?"

"I didn't know it, either," retorted Lee. "Otherwise I'd never signed the contract with you. I'm not a lumberman. You are supposed to be one. I think maybe you'd have done better sticking to cattle, which you appear to know something about. And I've a notion I'd have done better to make a deal with Wallace."

Radcliff gave a scoffing laugh. "A heck of a chance you'd have to make a deal with him!" he jeered. "You and I are in this thing together, Lee, and we've got to go through with it, but there's no use lying to ourselves about the T & W methods of financing and their trickery and cutting corners. I know what Wallace thinks of the T & W. He says it's coming through here just to milk the section, to make money out of it and give darn little in return. He's got a mighty poor opinion of the bunch backing the project. And we might as well admit he's right. Not that I give a darn either way. I'm out to even a few scores, and I aim to do it. But Wallace believes what he says, and because the C & P is backed by local capital, private subscription, he's all for 'em. He wouldn't sell you a stick of timber if you paid him twice what the C & P does, and you know it."

"Wallace is a crack-brained idealist," Lee snapped. "He's utterly impractical. He has an opportunity to get rich and throws it over. He's a fool. In this world the fittest survive. I've had to fight like blazes for everything I've got, and I don't expect anything to come easy. That part's all right. I'll keep on fighting, and I expect to win, no matter how faulty the tools I'm forced to work with. I repeat, Wallace is a fool!"

"Maybe," agreed Radcliff, his voice undergoing a subtle change. "But you know, Lee, it's possible to hate a man and still sort of admire him. In a way, Wallace is that kind of a jigger. He cares mighty little for money, or other folks' opinions, when they're set against what he figures to be right. You don't have to like that sort of a feller, but sometimes you find it sort of hard not to respect him."

Lee stared at him. "What the devil's the matter with you? Going soft?" he asked.

"No, I'm not," Radcliff disclaimed. "But when you get older, Lee, you kind of begin thinking about such things, and sometimes you wonder a bit. I've a notion you'll come to realize it, maybe, when you're getting along to my age."

"I doubt it," replied Lee. "As I said before, in this world only the fittest survive. I don't mean to say that a man always has to be off-color to succeed, but he does have to be hard and practical and not swayed by sentiment and foolish idealism. Well, be that is it may, it's sort of beside the point. I need bridge timbers and need them in a hurry. It's up to you to get them out faster than Wallace does. What methods you use is your own business. All I want is the stuff promised."

"You'll get it," Radcliff declared.

"I hope so," Lee said. "And remember, if you hope to even up the score with the folks who treated you like dirt in this business, you've got to get out more stuff than Wallace, and get it out faster."

Radcliff's face darkened and his eyes flashed resentfully.

"I'll get it," he repeated.

"Okay," said Lee, and left the saloon. Shortly afterward Radcliff also departed.

CHAPTER 6

Leaning back in the shadow, Hatfield pondered the peculiar mixture that was Bull Radcliff. He had gathered from Sheriff McGregor that Radcliff really believed Clark Wallace outsmarted him in a deal, tried to burn his sawmill and took a shot at him from the bushes. Just the same he admired Wallace's courage in standing up for what he considered right. Apparently little things like swindling, arson, and murder didn't particularly influence Radcliff's estimate of a man who had the guts to back his opinions. But Radcliff's casuistic philosophy didn't make for peace and order. It was results, not methods, that counted with him.

Quite likely Alton Lee also sensed that. Probably it was his reason for ending the discussion so abruptly. Doubtless Lee felt it would be wiser not to know too much about the methods Radcliff intended to employ.

Sheriff McGregor dropped in a little later and Hatfield called him over to have a drink.

"Well, how goes it?" he asked.

"Rather better than I'd expected," the sheriff replied. "A couple of rows, but nothing serious so far. I've a notion the boys are still a bit affected by what happened this morning. They're beginning to wonder if that explosion over by the bridge last week was another of the same sort. Nobody paid that one much mind. It just blew a hole in the ground and ripped up some rails and ties. They'd been doing considerable blasting in the vicinity and everybody figured it was just a stray stick that didn't go off with the rest of a charge."

"Sometimes a stick gets soaked and the water acts as a shield," Hatfield said. "Or perhaps the nitro is clotted and it takes a jolt in a specific spot to set it off."

"Reckon that's so," the sheriff agreed. "Anyhow, the boys are wondering, and a mite bothered. Can't say as I blame 'em. Not exactly pleasant not to know but that any minute the earth's liable to blow up under you."

Hatfield was willing to agree that the prospect did not tend to make for peace of mind.

"Well, I guess I'll be moving along," said the sheriff, sucking the drops from his mustache. "Want to drop in at the

Alhambra. Chuck Hooley and some of his bunch are there, and they're good at starting rukuses. Reckon Radcliff will be along soon to keep an eye on them, though. He sets considerable store by Hooley and don't want to see him in trouble."

"Hooley know the logging business?"

"He sure does," replied McGregor. "He's a funny sort, in some ways. Been around a lot, and done a lot of things. Was a cowhand for a while, I understand, and a card dealer. Was powder man for a big mine once, too. He can talk to you about dynamite. Reckon there isn't anything he doesn't know about it. He blows all Bull's stumps for him when he's clearing his cuttings to make grazing land, and does a bang-up job of it. He can jolt loose a chunk with half a stick of dynamite that other folks would have to use two or three whole sticks to move. I've watched him cutting the stuff in halves. Gave me the creeps, but he didn't pay it no mind. He's vicious and ornery, but one of those jiggers that does everything well that he set his hand to. Remember a while back, one of the hands at Radcliff's camp got a mighty bad slash with an ax. Was bleeding to death fast, I gather. Well, Hooley went to work on him, stopped the bleeding and had him in first class shape in no time. Doc McChesney said he couldn't have done a better job himself. Asked Hooley where he got the know-how. Hooley told him he worked as an orderly in a hospital once and picked up quite a few angles."

"Worked in a hospital?" Hatfield repeated.

"That's right," said the sheriff. "Over in Louisiana, I believe. Well, I've got to go. Thanks for the drink."

Hatfield enjoyed the boisterous gaiety of the payday celebration, but something after midnight he decided he'd better go to bed. He was very much on the alert as he made his way to the livery stable, although he hardly thought he might encounter trouble again. He reached his room without incident and immediately went to sleep.

Early the next morning he got the rig on Goldy and headed west through the defile that cut the hills, riding parallel to the railroad right-of-way. The C & P was double-tracking west from Cameron and he passed by a busy scene. Graders were at work. Groups of men were laying ties and spiking rails into place. Farther on he saw pick and shovel men busy grading the right-of-way ahead of the rails.

A little later he heard the chattering of

steam drills and reached a point where the defile was being widened for side tracks and passing tracks. Steam shovels puffed and their great mouthfuls of earth and stone thudded into the waiting cars to be borne away. At the base of a rocky wall, the shovels tore loose masses of talus, while higher up the wall, drill men bore holes to receive the dynamite charges that would bring down more of the cliff face.

Another mile and he saw the soaring web of timbering that was the bridge reaching out toward the far side of the gorge. From its bottom rose tall stone piers to which the ponderous girders would be anchored.

With an engineer's eyes, Hatfield saw at a glance that the bridge was the key to the race for the Pass. Any prolonged delay here would be fatal. The same, of course, applied to the T & W project. And he realized the importance of the role played by the rival lumber camps. No wonder Alton Lee was decidedly beside himself over the failure of Radcliff to provide suitable material as swiftly as Clark Wallace apparently was doing.

Hatfield was still some little distance from the bridge, and had turned toward it from the trail, when a man carrying a rifle stepped out and held up his hand.

"That'll be far enough, cowboy," he called, not unpleasantly. "Sorry, but we have strict orders not to allow anybody to come close to the bridge."

"Been having trouble?" Hatfield asked as he pulled Goldy to a halt.

"Well, no, not exactly, I guess," the guard replied hesitantly. "But after what happened in town yesterday we're on the lookout for anything."

"A good notion," Hatfield agreed. With a nod to the guard, he turned Goldy and rode back the way he had come. He had seen all he cared to see, for the time being.

Upon reaching the eastern mouth of the defile, Hatfield headed north by slightly west. Here the hills fell away, but the gorge was even deeper and almost as wide. Soon he saw the webwork of the T & W bridge looming against the sky.

As he neared the right-of-way he was again halted, this time very peremptorily, by two men holding rifles at the ready. They were hard characters, he decided, and of a more alert and intelligent look than usual with men who took up that sort of work. He merely nodded and turned Goldy east. The suspicious eyes of the guards followed his progress until he was out of sight. Later he passed several more of like calibre, but he was out on the prairie and none spoke to him. Finally he reached the broad Coronado Trail and turned north by east. Shortly the trail entered the hills and ran between long slopes covered with timber growth.

With an upward trend the trail wound on. The timber flanked it on either side, with the huge brown trunks forming cathedral aisles carpeted with the rich brown fallen leaves.

But as Hatfield rode on, a sound began to blunt the sharp edge of the stillness, a click and mutter that grew to a deep rumble. Around a bend rolled a line of big freighting wagons loaded with ties and ponderous beams. Riding at the head of the train was Chuck Hooley.

Hatfield reined aside to let the wagons pass. Hooley came abreast of him, scowled, but did not speak. Hatfield studied his bad-tempered face. It was heavy-featured, but not a stupid face. Hooley's eyes were small, set deep in his head, but brilliant. His nose was well formed, his mouth a cruel slit, the lips seeming to pull back hard against the teeth. Hatfield wondered if he ever smiled. However, the slightly receding chin belied the grimness of the rest of his face. An able man, but at the bottom a weak one, Hatfield decided. He sensed also that Hooley knew he was weak and strove to cover up the weakness with a mask of blustering arrogance.

Hooley rode on, and did not turn. The wagon drivers evidently recalled Hatfield from the day on the station platform but apparently harbored no resentment. They grinned and nodded. Several waved their hands. Hatfield wondered just how popular Hooley really was with the rank and file of Radcliff's hands.

As he rode on Hatfield began hearing another sound, the querulous whine of a sawmill and a steady rhythmic clicking of ax-steel on wood. He studied the trees that encroached the trail. They were burr oak. He realized that he was passing Bull Radcliff's holding.

The sound died out behind him and followed another period of silence. Then again the rhythmic ring of axes and the rasp of saws biting into the tough forest giants. Now the trees on either side were live oaks. He was on Clark Wallace's land.

Suddenly a long-drawn call sounded clear and musical, "Ti-i-im-m-ber!"

There was a crackling, a rustle and swish

that crescendoed to a rushing roar which ended in a mighty thud.

"That was a big one," he told Goldy. "Must be getting pretty close to where Wallace is cutting."

A few minutes later he rounded a bend and a scene of bustling activity unfolded before his eyes. He was on the edge of a wide cutting. Ax blades flashed, rasping saws shimmered back and forth. Men moved about and shouted orders. Again the long-drawn call rang out. Another great tree leaned slowly and majestically to the accompaniment of splitting fibres, gathered speed as it left the perpendicular and rushed downward, branches thrashing, leaves showering and glinting in the sunshine.

The loggers were lithe, sinewy men who moved alertly, mostly fresh-faced young fellows who chattered gaily among themselves. Evidently they enjoyed their work and were satisfied with the man they worked for. Hatfield smiled slightly as he hooked one long leg comfortably over the saddle horn, rolled a cigarette and smoked with enjoyment, his strangely colored eyes all kindness.

The Lone Wolf liked such scenes. Men taking pleasure from worthwhile chores, doing hard toil with cheerfulness and content. They and their kind were what Texas needed. They were of the breed that won the West and would make a great state ever greater.

It was because there were such people in Texas, and more coming, that he was in the Rangers for so much longer than he had originally intended. He joined the famous corps at the behest of Captain McDowell, who didn't want to see the son of his old friend ride the vengeance trail alone and very likely end up finding himself on the wrong side of the law. Hatfield had kept up his studies and expected some day to be an engineer. But Ranger service presented so many opportunities to serve worthwhile folks and make the way a little easier for them, that he had been, and still was loath to sever connections with the famed "Gentlemen in the White Hats" who brought law and order to a land that before their coming had known neither.

A crew of axmen approached another tall tree, glancing upward, shrewdly estimating its height, and decided on the direction in which it would fall. The trunk had already been girdled with a white line to guide the axmen. Two stepped forward, their heavy double-bitted axes slanting over their shoulders. They planted their feet wide apart and swung the glittering blades in perfect unison.

The accurately timed strokes rang against the wood. The axmen levered their blades free and struck again. A broad white chip flew through the air. A deep wound appeared in the tree trunk.

Again the axmen swung, the keen blades biting deep.

There was a crashing roar, a mushrooming cloud of yellowish smoke, and a shriek of agony and terror.

CHAPTER 7

It took Hatfield seconds to master his frantic horse, who was dancing and rearing and snorting with fright. By the time he got the big sorrel under control, the smoke cloud had cleared. One whole side of the tree trunk was blown away. Fragments of wood were scattered about. The two axmen lay prone on the ground, one very still, his head twisted on his shoulders at a horrid angle. The other man was writhing and moaning with pain. Men were running toward the scene of the disaster, shouting and screaming.

Hatfield whipped to the ground and ran forward. He knelt beside the injured man, saw that his left leg was broken, the flesh gashed and shredded. Blood was pouring from the wound. Jerking the handkerchief from about his neck, he swiftly improvised a tourniquet, using a gun barrel for a rod, and stanched the appalling flow of blood.

"Another handkerchief, two or three of them," he called over his shoulder. "And there's a roll of bandage and a jar of salve in my left saddlebag. Get them, somebody. It's all right, Goldy," he told the trembling horse.

He treated and bandaged the ghastly wound as well as he could, set the broken bone and splinted it with strips of wood the loggers speedily hewed out with their axes.

"Make a stretcher with poles thrust through coat sleeves," he ordered. He himself lifted the wounded man to the improvised stretcher.

"Take him to the bunkhouse and put him to bed," he told the workers. "He should be all right till we can get the doctor here."

He stood up, his face bleak, his eyes the cold gray of frosted steel, and for a moment stared at the riven tree trunk.

Hatfield spotted the slight form of Clark Wallace hurrying to the scene.

"What happened?" the lumberman demanded.

"Some sidewinder bored a hole in the trunk where the ring denoted the height for cutting, planted dynamite in it and plugged it up," Hatfield replied tersely. "When the axmen began chopping they set off the charge. Killed one man, smashed up another."

Clark Wallace swore a bitter oath. "More devil's work," he said in a shaking voice. "Seems to be no end to it. Blast Bull Radcliff!"

"Hold it!" Hatfield told him sternly. "There's no proof Radcliff had anything to do with it. Don't go making accusations you can't back up. You did that yesterday, and was sorry afterward."

Wallace flushed. "I — I reckon you're right," he said.

Hatfield turned his bleak gaze on the muttering loggers. "And what I just said goes for the rest of you," he told them. "Understand! Keep a tight latigo on your jaws till you know what you're talking about."

There was a ring of authority in the deep voice that stilled the mutterings. Somehow, this tall, level-eyed cowhand had taken complete charge of the situation.

Hatfield turned back to Wallace. "Send somebody to town for the doctor," he directed. "I think the other one will pull through if he survives the shock and loss of blood. We should be able to save his leg. And notify the sheriff. Don't move that poor devil's body till he gets here. He'll want to hold an inquest and it's best for him to see things just as they happened.

Cover it with a blanket and set a man to watch it."

Hatfield beckoned the workers to gather around him. "Before you lay an ax to another tree, examine all that have been ringed," he directed. "I doubt if a second one has been loaded, but don't take any chances. And, Wallace, I think you'd better set a patrol riding your property, just in case somebody has some more notions to put into effect."

"I will," Wallace promised. "Incidentally, that's what I want to talk to you about. But come on and we'll have something to eat first.

"And you fellows knock off for a couple of hours," he told his hands. "Line your bellies good, and I'll break out a couple of bottles and everybody can have a snort. That should help."

After eating, Hatfield, with Wallace's guidance, looked over the camp, which was well appointed. He noted with interest the long trough of a flume that extended up the slope of the mountain and on the downward side vanished over the lip of the little plateau that provided the camp site. Wallace pointed to it with pride.

"That's how I send my logs down to the valley where I have a loading station and a sawmill," he explained. "The flume passes by the western tip of Radcliff's holdings. It saves me miles of expensive hauling and is also a tremendous saving of time. I only have to haul from the valley over to the C & P spur."

"Where do you get the water?" Hatfield asked as he gazed at the rushing stream that brimmed the trough.

Wallace gestured upward to where the long slope ended in a cliff some seventy feet in height.

"A natural reservoir up there," he said. "A deep cup walled about by cliffs. There are evidently big springs gushing up through the rock, with a subterranean drain at the bottom of the cup. The cup never overflows except after an unusually long and hard rain. It was made to order for lumbering operations. I recognized its worth when I looked over the ground before buying. That's where I have a big advantage over Radcliff. He has to move his timber altogether by hauling."

"Your whole project mighty nigh depends on the flume, eh?" Hatfield commented, gazing thoughtfully upward at the beetling line of low cliffs curving out of sight through the trees that flanked the barren slope above the camp.

"That's right," Wallace admitted.

Hatfield nodded, still gazing upward. Wallace was silent for a moment. Then he said, "Hatfield, here's what I want to talk to you about. I want to offer you a job. I'll pay you more than you can get on a ranch and the work will be easier, and, which naturally appeals to a cowboy, it will consist largely of riding. I need somebody trustworthy to patrol my property and prevent just such things as happened today. I've been thinking of it ever since I saw you in action there on the station platform. This isn't the first trouble I've had."

He gestured to a blackened spot of considerable size that scarred the plateau a few score yards distant.

"My storeroom used to stand there," he explained. "It was burned one night. Twice the trough of the flume was blown up between here and the level ground below. I was shot once, from ambush. I lost valuable time repairing the flume — I have men guarding it now. There is a systematic campaign to drive me out of business."

Hatfield nodded, and proffered a comment that was rather a statement of fact than a question. "And due to the lumber you supply them, the C & P is forging ahead in the race to Alpine Pass?"

"That's so," replied Wallace. "If they had to haul from back east they would be at a disadvantage. What do you say about the job?"

Hatfield did not answer for a moment. The proposition appealed to him. It would give him an excuse for hanging around the section, and would allow him a freedom of movement a job of riding for one of the neighboring spreads would not afford.

When he arrived at Cameron, Jim Hatfield's intention was to announce himself as a Texas Ranger, confident that the prestige of the famous silver star set on a silver circle, the badge of the Rangers, would be sufficient to prevent the bickering between the rival railroads from erupting into open violence. But the events of the past thirty-six hours had changed his mind for him. He found himself confronted by a sinister mystery. Granted that the explosion in Cameron the day before was possibly a freak accident, what happened today at Wallace's camp was no accident. This was positive intent.

The objective, of course, was to slow up Wallace's lumbering operations. Today a man had been killed and another perhaps crippled for life. Unless whoever responsible was run down, and quickly, undoubtedly other men would die.

"Wallace," he said, "I'll take the chore."

The young lumberman drew a deep breath of relief. "I feel better," he declared. "I've a notion you'll be able to spot anything off-color that's going on, and able to cope with it, no matter what it is."

Hatfield smiled slightly. "I hope so," he said, "and now suppose you saddle up and show me over the property."

Wallace got his horse and they rode over the lumberman's holdings, which were extensive.

"Good timber here," Hatfield observed. "The completion of the railroad project won't end your operation. Plenty of stuff here you can ship to the open market. I'd like to ride up this north slope to the reservoir and look it over."

"Okay," Wallace agreed. "We can reach the crest from this side. No cliffs on the north."

Half an hour later found them on the edge of a placid sheet of blue water something less than a third of a mile in circumference and almost circular in shape. The perpendicular wall of the southern cliffs rose to about a dozen feet above the surface of the water.

"She's deep," Hatfield remarked. "I've a notion this cup was once a volcanic blowhole, maybe a million years or so back."

"Couldn't say as to that," Wallace replied, "but it sure came in handy for me. Let's be getting back to the camp. It's almost supper time."

When they arrived at the camp they found Sheriff McGregor and Doc McChesney. The old frontier doctor gave Hatfield a peculiar look and his white mustache twitched slightly as the sheriff introduced them.

"You saved that young hellion's life," he said to the Lone Wolf, jerking his thumb toward the bunkhouse. "Saved his leg, too, for that matter. Barring complications, which I don't expect, he should be back on the job in six weeks. I changed the bandage and put on more and heavier splints. Be back to see him tomorrow."

The sheriff's face was grim as Hatfield gave him a detailed account of what had happened in the clearing.

"Some sidewinder hereabouts is sure due to stretch rope, or eat lead," he predicted. "Either way is okay with me. And I'll be all ready to handle the chore."

"Got to catch your rabbit 'fore you cook it," Hatfield observed.

"I got a notion the trap's already being built," the doctor remarked. "Well, I'll be getting back to town," he added.

"I'll help you hitch up," Hatfield offered.

Inside the stable, where there was nobody around, McChesney again shook hands with Hatfield.

"What are you doing down here, Doc?" the Ranger asked. "You hop around like a flea with two dogs to look after."

"Oh, things were getting too peaceful up in the Panhandle, folks were getting too darn healthy, and I was getting too poor," McChesney replied. "What are you doing here, Jim?"

"Thought I was here to take it sort of easy for a spell, but it looks like I was mistaken," Hatfield answered wryly. "I should be up in the Panhandle where you were."

"And you'd be plumb miserable," McChesney declared. "If you ain't in the middle of some trouble you ain't happy. How's McDowell?"

"He's okay," Hatfield replied. "I'll tell him I saw you. And, Doc, I'll be in town to see you shortly. I'd like for you to give me the lowdown on a few folks hereabouts."

"Be glad to help any way I can," said the doctor. "Take care of yourself, Jim."

Hatfield watched him drive away and then went in to eat supper with Wallace and the sheriff.

CHAPTER 8

Several days passed peacefully enough. Hatfield patrolled the property ceaselessly, familiarizing himself with the terrain, trying to figure out where the next blow might fall. He inspected the sawmill and landing station and was favorably impressed by the efficiency of both. Wallace had a very short haul to contend with. The railroad had run a spur out from the Cameron yards and there were always strings of empties waiting to receive the beams and crossties. Close to the mill was a dry kiln in which the massive beams were quickly dried and seasoned.

Hatfield decided quickly that the flume was the most vulnerable part of the lumbering equipment. If it were tampered with, irritating delay would ensue. A nuisance value for anybody seeking to hold up the work. He insisted that the men patrolling the long trough should be mounted and he gave them orders to shoot on sight.

And then, without warning, disaster

struck. It was but little after daybreak of a clear morning. Hatfield was watering Goldy at the flume. The loggers were washing up for breakfast. Wallace was already busy in his little office.

Suddenly a coughing explosion rent the air. Hatfield glanced up the slope, from which the sound had come. A cloud of smoke was gushing from the face of the cliff. The echoes of the explosion were followed by a mighty crackling and crashing and an ominous roar.

Through the eddying smoke cloud burst a wall of water racing down the slope at terrific speed. Its thunder shook the air. Bushes and shrubs were torn from the earth and hurled skyward. Boulders started from their beds of centuries and bounded down the slope.

Hatfield's voice rang out above the increasing uproar and the frightened cries of the loggers. "Get in the clear! Hightail for the timber! Move! It'll sweep the camp clean!"

He gathered up Goldy's bridle and prepared to join the demoralized rush for shelter. Abruptly he remembered the injured logger who lay helpless in the big bunkhouse.

"Trail, Goldy! Get in the clear!" he

shouted, giving the sorrel a resounding slap on his glossy haunch.

As Goldy streaked away, snorting indignantly, Hatfield whirled and raced to the bunkhouse. He dove through the doorway, gathered the injured man in his arms, blankets and all, and bounded at top speed across the clearing. The wall of water, its curling crest higher than a tall man's head, was less than a hundred yards distant. Before Hatfield could reach the timberline it was upon him. Water sloshed about his ankles, rose instantly to his knees, his thighs, his waist. The main body of the flood roared toward him like a ravening monster. He knew that if the full force of the water struck him, both he and his helpless burden would be swept over the lip of the plateau and pounded to pulp on the stones below. He struggled on madly, fighting the pull of the undertow, reeling, staggering, his breath coming in hoarse gasps.

With the swirling current tearing at his shoulders he made a final prodigious effort. He was all but swept off his feet. The curving crest of the main flood hung over him. As he reached the tree line it broke upon him, hurling him to the ground, then lifting him in liquid arms that clutched like the tentacles of an octopus. His out-reaching hand gripped the trunk of a small sapling and he strained with every ounce of his strength to hold his own. Just as his grip was torn from the trunk a dozen hands reached him as the loggers stormed to the rescue. By main strength they dragged him from the flood and into the shallower water that swirled amid the tree trunks, its force broken by the obstacles it encountered. A moment later all were in safety.

Hatfield, gasping for breath himself, grinned down at the half drowned man he still gripped to his chest.

"If this didn't kill you, son, I figure nothing will," he chuckled.

The injured logger coughed some of the water out of his lungs and grinned wanly in return.

"I'll live," he panted. "The good Lord wouldn't let me cash in after the way you risked your own life to save me. That wouldn't be right at all."

The flood subsided quickly. The loggers returned to the clearing to learn the extent of the damage. They found the camp a mess. Some of the buildings were turned on their foundations. Their furnishings were a splintered tangle. Much of the flume had been uprooted and hurled aside.

Deep gullies were scored in the surface of the plateau and tree trunks, displaced boulders and uprooted brush were scattered about in every direction.

Fortunately, the big stable stood well over to one side and had escaped with nothing worse than a wetting. None of the horses were lost.

"There's nothing here that can't be put back into shape in a hurry," Hatfield told Wallace. "Let's get up to the reservoir and see what happened there. I don't like the looks of it. You'll notice there's no water coming down."

They clambered up the muddy slope until they reached the base of the cliff. A great hole gaped in the retaining wall about ten feet above the ground. Hatfield examined it with increasing interest.

"There's a fault in the cliff here," he pointed out to Wallace. "A strata of much softer rock, worn thin, no doubt, by the action of the water throughout the ages. It was there the hellion planted his explosive to blow a hole in the wall. At any other spot he couldn't have done it. Very interesting!"

Wallace stared at the seamed and broken cliff face.

"I never would have noticed it," he said.

"It all looks the same to me."

"The average person wouldn't notice it," Hatfield replied. "That's what makes it interesting. It requires more than a little knowledge of geology, and petrology, the science of rocks, to notice a condition like this, and to appreciate its possibilities."

Wallace glanced at him in a bewildered way. Hatfield meanwhile was staring down the slope, his mouth set in a hard line, a perplexed expression in his green eyes. He shook his black head, turned back to the cliff face.

"Let's try and get through that hole and take a look at what's inside," he suggested.

They managed, with considerable difficulty, to climb up the jagged face of the rock and worm their way through the rift to the inner edge. From their point of vantage they could survey the circular cup of the emptied reservoir. They saw that the spring which fed it gushed, quite high up, through the north wall. The bottom of the cup was now practically free of water. Directly under where they stood was a wide swirling pool into which the stream from the spring flowed. As they watched, the agitated surface of the pool maintained a constant level.

"The shock of the explosion perhaps

widened a little the opening in the bottom of the cup that provides the drain," Hatfield said. "It carries off the water now as swiftly as it flows from the spring."

"And from the looks of it, the reservoir will never fill up again!" Wallace exclaimed. "Well, I reckon this very nearly finishes my lumber business, so far as making anything like a decent profit is concerned. And also about kills the C & P's chance of winning the race to Alpine Pass. I'll have a much longer haul than Radcliff. But there's nothing else to do. I can't get water for my flume any more."

Hatfield had been studying the spring and estimating the conditions of the cup floor and the opening through the wall. He turned to the despondent lumberman. "Oh, yes you can," he replied cheerfully. "The worst you're facing is a little delay, and we'll make that up by working double shifts for a while. We ride to town pronto and telegraph for a couple of big hydraulic rams. The C & P will see to it that they're rushed here. They're all you need to take care of the situation. You'll notice that the level of the spring is considerably greater than that of the bottom of the cup. With the rams you can easily raise the required water to this hole in the wall here and feed your flume. I can install the rams for you.

Start your man repairing the flume and getting it back in place. Come on, feller, we're riding!"

With Wallace chattering his relief and thanks to Hatfield, they scrambled back down the slope and headed for Cameron. Once there they immediately went to the telegraph office. With the help of the C & P officials the arrangements for getting the rams were quickly made, including all necessary materials.

"We'll rush them here by special train," the division superintendent assured them. "What in blazes will happen next, I wonder? Once this chore of building is finished, I think I'll resign, go out in the desert and spend my time at some nice peaceable occupation like trapping rattlesnakes."

"Rattlesnakes aren't so bad," observed Hatfield. "They never fang if you just leave them alone. Which is more than you can say for the garden variety of snakes operating in this section. Come on, Wallace, let's go see the sheriff. I want to listen to him swear when we tell him what happened. By the way, anything gone wrong hereabouts of late?"

"Anything gone wrong!" snorted the super. "Hadn't you heard? There was another dynamite explosion out near the bridge day before yesterday. Blew an engine and a crane off the track, killed two men and hurt half a dozen others."

Hatfield stared at him. "Thought you were keeping a close watch on everything," he observed.

"Tarnation, we are!" the super exploded. "But it doesn't seem to do a darn bit of good. With every rail-length of the right-of-way constantly patrolled, still somebody manages to sneak in and plant a charge of explosive under the tracks and set it off. A little more of this and we're licked. Men are beginning to quit, and I don't blame them. And those who are working are so jittery they're not getting half done they should. For God's sake, Wallace, don't you let us down or we are finished."

"We won't if you get that equipment here in a hurry," Hatfield promised for the lumberman.

"I'll burn up the wires till it's on the way," the super promised.

"Okay," Hatfield nodded. "Come on, Clark, let's go see the sheriff."

As they walked to McGregor's office, Hatfield remarked, "Somebody hereabouts sure has a liking for dynamite. And knows how to use it," he added. "That chore on the flume was a lulu. Took plenty of know-how to figure that one out. Whoever did it figured correctly that the flow of water from the spring was practically static with the flow from the subterranean drain. Lower the level of the water in the cup, and the level would stand at that point unless there happened to come a prolonged and heavy rain, which isn't often in this country. I was plain outsmarted by that one, too. I was concentrating on the flume and never thought to keep an eye on the source of supply. But somebody noticed that fault in the cliff and realized what it could very likely mean."

"I'd never have believed Radcliff was capable of figuring out such a thing," commented Wallace.

Hatfield glanced down at him. "He wasn't, isn't, and never would be, I'm willing to bet money on that," he said.

The visit to the sheriff was productive of little other than explosive profanity. McGregor swore in weary disgust when told of the latest outrage.

"I don't know what it's all about or who's responsible," he declared, "but I do know there are quite a few folks getting the notion of lynching Bull Radcliff."

"I don't think lynching Radcliff would

solve the problem," Hatfield remarked quietly, "and as chief peace officer of this county, it's up to you to prevent such a thing from happening."

"You don't need to tell me my duty," growled the sheriff. "There'll be no lynchings hereabouts if I can prevent it, and I think I can. But the railroad folks are after me hot and heavy. The T & W people have been having trouble, too. Somebody set fire to their roundhouse the other night. If Alton Lee hadn't been on the job and discovered the blaze before it got really started, the whole shebang would have gone up in smoke and a number of locomotives would have been ruined. They swear the C & P crowd is responsible, in retaliation for the trouble they've been having. I'm beginning to be of the opinion they're all liars, only I can't prove it. If Bull Radcliff is taken out of the picture, then who the devil is responsible?"

"Sometimes hired hands get out of order without the Boss knowing about it," Hatfield observed evasively.

"Uh-huh, I've thought of that," agreed the sheriff. "Personal grudges and so on."

While Wallace was busy contracting for the delivery of some needed supplies, Hatfield dropped in on Doc McChesney. The old doctor broke out a bottle and glasses and seated his visitor in an easy chair with his refreshment within reach.

"Well, what's on your mind?" he asked. "I know you didn't come here just to pass the time of day."

"Doctors know everything," Hatfield replied with a smile. "I just want to get the lowdown on some folks hereabouts. For instance, what do you know about Chuck Hooley, Bull Radcliff's logging boss?"

"Not overly much," McChesney said. "I know he's mean as the dickens, or pretends to be. He sets up to be tough and salty and a roughneck, but sometimes I wonder. I've talked with him a couple of times, when I was patching him up after he'd been in a shindig, and somehow I got the impression he isn't exactly what he seems to want folks to believe. Can't help but feel that once upon a time he was something quite different. That's not so unusual out here, you know. Sometimes jiggers get off on the wrong foot somewhere and have to trail their twine. Then they try to wipe out the past and become something different. Could be with Hooley."

"Think he has education to amount to anything?"

"Wouldn't be surprised if he has," Doc

answered. "Sometimes he lets a word slip that doesn't tie in with the rest of his talk."

Hatfield nodded thoughtfully. "And what about Bull Radcliff?"

"A stubborn old shorthorn," McChesney instantly replied. "When he gets his head set on something, nothing can pry him loose. He's the sort that won't back down even when he knows it's the right and sensible thing to do. Take the row he's in with the other cowmen over the coming of the railroad. I'm convinced that Bull realizes now that the C & P building through here is to the advantage of everybody, but get him to admit it? Not a chance! He knows darn well, too, that Clark Wallace made a perfectly legitimate deal with him for that timber land. Wallace was gambling on the road coming through, and won, that's all. But Bull had to see it as a deep-dyed scheme to flim-flam him out of a valuable holding. Just because Wallace was a mite smarter than he was. He took that contract to supply the T & W with timber not because he needed the money, which he don't, but just out of pure contrariness and a get-even spirit. What to do with the likes of him I don't know."

"I don't either — yet," Hatfield admitted. They talked for a while about past events. Finally Hatfield glanced at the clock and stood up.

"Promised to meet Wallace over by the railroad station," he said.

"I'll walk with you," McChesney announced. "The afternoon train is just about due. Want to see if I've got any mail."

The train was just pulling in when they reached the station. Hatfield spotted Clark Wallace farther down the platform and they sauntered in his direction.

A few passengers descended from the coaches. A trainman came down the steps bearing a heavy suitcase. He reached up a hand to assist someone to the platform. A moment later a girl stepped lightly from the coach.

She was dark and slender with softly curling brown hair, wide blue eyes and red lips. Her cheeks were creamily sun golden and there were a few freckles powdering the straight bridge of her little tip-tilted nose. Altogether, a very pretty girl, Hatfield thought.

Standing nearby was Clark Wallace. Hatfield saw his eyes widen as he gazed at the girl. She, at the same moment, picked up her suitcase and started toward the street. She stepped on a pebble that rolled under her foot and stumbled off balance. Clark Wallace leaped forward and caught her just as she was about to fall. She clung to his arm, laughed merrily and flashed him a grateful smile. Wallace released her and his face flushed scarlet. He opened his lips to speak. But at that moment a man shouldered in front of him, ignoring him as if he didn't exist. It was Bull Radcliff.

The girl gave a glad little cry and flung herself into Bull's arms.

"Daddy!" she exclaimed delightedly. "Oh, but it's good to see you again after all these months!"

Radcliff held her close for a moment, then he picked up her suitcase and turned toward a waiting buckboard. The girl, still holding fast to his big arm, flashed another dazzling smile over her shoulder to Clark Wallace.

Wallace stood like a man dazed, staring after her.

Doc gazed after the departing buckboard. "Reckon Helen takes after her mom more than her pop in size and good looks," he commented. "She sure don't bear much resemblance to Bull. Imagine she's back home to stay now — been away to school."

Wallace wasn't very good company during the ride back to camp. He was distrait and his answers were random. Suddenly, however, he burst out. "How in blazes could an old shorthorn like Bull Radcliff have a daughter like that?"

Hatfield shook with laughter. "Johann Mendel explains it fairly well in his *Research Upon Hybridization*," he said smiling. "Ever read it?"

"No!" snorted Wallace, "and I don't even know what you're talking about, but wasn't she a wonder?"

"A very charming girl," Hatfield agreed.

CHAPTER 9

With the C & P Railroad vitally interested and pushing matters, the hydraulic rams were quickly obtained and hauled from Cameron to Wallace's lumber camp. Jim Hatfield supervised the job of installation and the big rams were speedily set up and working. They were placed at the edge of the whirlpool at the bottom of the cup.

"They work automatically and will keep on operating indefinitely so long as they aren't tampered with," Hatfield told the lumberman. "They'll give you all the water you need."

Wallace was profoundly grateful. "You've saved my business for me, and I won't forget it," he declared. "Your pay envelope will show just a mite how much I appreciate what you've done for me, and if the C & P Railroad does the right thing, they'll vote you a block of stock. You saved their bacon for them, too."

"Maybe," Hatfield chuckled, "but they're still a long ways from getting it fried!"

"Think they'll win the race to the Pass?"

"If you can keep on shoving them the stuff, I believe they will," Hatfield replied. "But," he added thoughtfully, "I've a notion they're wishing about now that they'd decided to build that bridge of steel instead of wood. Of course the idea, aside from the economic factor, was to make speed. When they learned the T & W had made a deal with Radcliff for timber right on the spot, they were afraid that if they took time to have steel fabricated and shipped here, the T & W would forge ahead. Guess they didn't figure on the complications that have developed. Well, the fat's in the fire, now. They've got a third of the bridge built and they'll have to go through with it. You're just about the key figure in a multi-million dollar enterprise, Wallace."

"And it makes me nervous as the devil! Hatfield, is there anything you don't know all about?"

"Yes, several things I'd very much like to know all about," Hatfield replied grimly.

Wallace looked puzzled, but decided it was useless to ask questions.

"I suppose we'd better keep those rams guarded all the time," he observed.

"I hardly think whoever is raising the devil hereabouts will bother with a picayunish business like tampering with the rams," Hatfield said. "It would cause only a slight temporary delay. What we've got to try and figure out is how, where, and when they'll strike next."

"Tarnation you give me the creeps!" Wallace exclaimed. "And you really think whoever it is will try again?"

Hatfield shrugged his broad shoulders. "A rattlesnake doesn't stop fanging when he misses his first stroke, that is if what he's after is still around and kicking," he replied. "I figure whoever started this business is in it to the finish. After the extremes they've already gone to, you can't expect them to shut up shop now. You might as well be on the outlook for more trouble, because you're going to get it, if you can't forestall it. That's my chore, I reckon, sort of what you hired me for. So you go ahead with your lumbering and I'll see what I can do to tangle the sidewinder's twine for him."

Suddenly a distant rumbling shook the air, followed by a second shock, and a third, apparently coming from the southeast.

"Now what the dickens?" Hatfield said.

"Oh, that's nothing," said Wallace. "It's just Bull Radcliff blowing out stumps. He's efficient, I'll have to say that for him. As soon as he cuts a stretch, he immediately begins clearing it up for grassland."

"Seems everybody in this section has a liking for dynamite," Hatfield remarked morosely. "I'm getting so I jump every time I hear a stick go off."

Despite his conviction that it was hardly likely anybody would meddle with the rams, Hatfield spent considerable time around the reservoir. He decided that it was the weak spot in the fabric of the lumbering project. And if there were the potentials of trouble here, he had an uneasy premonition that whoever had the acumen to recognize the one spot where it was possible to blow a hole through the cliff might discover them. If such a hazard existed, it was vital that he should learn it first.

The formation was peculiar. To the south and to the east were the sheer cliffs. On the north a gentle slope ran up to the lip of what had once been the ancient volcanic blow hole. But on the west a long, rather steep slope flung upward to form a rounded skyline.

While patrolling the timberlands, Hatfield did not neglect to practice his usual caution and to constantly study the terrain where he happened to be riding. The fact that no further attempt against his life had been made since the failure of the initial try with the pile of rails in Cameron did not lull him into any feeling of false security. He took no chances.

One day, while riding the western slope near the south wall of the reservoir, he thought he saw movement far up the slope, a drifting shadow that could be a horseman riding near the rimrock. He did not turn his head but slanted his eyes up the sag. A moment later he saw it again, a flicker of movement amid the thinner upper growth. Then a third time, and he knew he was not mistaken. There was somebody up there in the shadow of the crags, apparently pacing him, and nobody had any business being there.

Unless the mysterious rider worked his way farther down the slope he was beyond anything like accurate rifle range, but there was no guarantee he would not be able to shift his position to one of better vantage without being observed from below. Hatfield quickly developed an unpleasant feeling of approaching danger. He was in very much the position of a setting quail.

Directly ahead the growth bristled up tall and thick for several hundred yards. For a space he would be invisible to anybody on the upper slope. The slope was not so steep that a powerful horse like Goldy could not make it. Hatfield quickened the sorrel's gait and was soon behind the sheltering growth. At a favorable spot he turned Goldy up the slope.

For about half the distance to the rimrock he rode. Then he dismounted, left the sorrel and climbed swiftly on foot.

"If that jigger keeps on being as careless as he was a little bit ago, I should be able to get a look at him," he told himself. "And, with a little luck, drop a loop on him. May get a line on who is kicking up the trouble in this section."

With ever increasing caution he worked his way up the slope until he was above the spot where he had seen the mysterious rider. Then, after pausing to peer and listen, he stole south. Through the straggle of growth he could catch occasional glimpses of the reservoir cliffs and was able to estimate pretty closely just where he had noted the drifting shadow. He could see now that from the elevation there was an excellent view of the base of the slope for a considerable distance. A careful prowler could see everything that went on below and still be secure from observation.

"And if I hadn't spotted the hellion, I'd

have quite likely leaned against the hot end of a passing slug," he muttered as he began easing down the slope, taking care not to make the slightest sound, pausing every few steps to strain his ears and search the ground ahead with a carping gaze.

But there was no sign of movement amid the shadows under the growth, and only the faint rustling of leaves in the wind and an occasional bird call broke the silence. Hatfield began to wonder if the prowler, whoever he was, had ridden on to the north.

Not likely, he decided. If he really hoped to get in a shot he would be much more apt to remain where he had a clear view of the reservoir and the open space to the south. If he was still here, he doubtless had moved farther down the slope. Hatfield continued his cautious descent.

He was half-way down the sag when he saw, a dozen yards or so in front, something bulky behind a ledge of rock, a ledge that provided excellent cover. He halted, staring intently at the shadow object, which, as his eyes grew more accustomed to the gloom under the thick brush, assumed the outlines of a kneeling man. He could just make out something projecting over the ledge, doubtless a rifle barrel. The fellow was waiting his chance.

A feeling of hot wrath welled in Hatfield's breast. His hand gripped the butt of his gun. He would be perfectly justified in shooting the snake-blooded killer without warning. But instantly his hand fell away from the big Colt. He was a peace officer, and a peace officer must announce himself and his intentions. That was the code of the Rangers.

And there were other considerations involved. If he could take the fellow alive, he might glean some valuable information. Hatfield was pretty well convinced that a single man, a man of ability and cold courage, was behind the sinister happenings in the section, but he was not absolutely sure. Should he drill a slug through the crouching drygulcher, he might just cash in some underling and leave the real menace to go free. No, he'd take a desperate chance, shooting as a last resort. Silently as an Indian he moved farther down, keeping well under cover, testing the ground ahead with each step before he trusted his weight on it.

The form ahead did not move, but apparently kept staring at something far down the slope. Hatfield, his own view obscured by the tangle of brush, grew de-

106

cidedly uneasy. Perhaps Clark Wallace might be the intended victim. Wallace spent considerable time around the camp and at the head of the flume. It could be Wallace and not himself the drygulcher had in mind. He decided to instantly draw and shoot should the shadowy slimness that he judged was a rifle barrel move as if to line with a target. Holding his breath, he crept forward a few more feet. Now he was certain it was a man crouched there, a man with a hat pulled down on his head, hunched over the ledge. Another yard and he'd risk a spring. Then with his hands on the fellow's neck, he had little doubt as to the outcome. He glided forward, crouched, his muscles tensing for the leap. His glance swept over the shadowy figure.

Abruptly he relaxed his position a little, his puzzled gaze fixed on the drygulcher's right foot. It was twisted around until the toe of the boot pointed almost backward, an impossible position for a normal foot. And he abruptly realized what he had ignored in the absorption of stalking the quarry. The crouching figure had not moved as much as a finger from the time he had first spotted it! Was the fellow dead, or injured and unconscious? That impossibly twisted foot hinted at one or the other.

Hatfield crouched motionless, debating the situation. Finally he drew his left gun and with his right hand groped about carefully till his fingers encountered a small stone. He tossed the pebble at the crouching figure.

He saw the stone strike squarely in the middle of the rounded back with a soft little sound and drop to the ground. The figure did not move.

Hatfield's scalp prickled; he felt cold between his shoulder blades as he realized the truth. The thing wasn't a man at all, but an artfully contrived dummy. Doubtless the real drygulcher was hidden nearby with a gun trained on the spot where Hatfield would materialize when he attacked the motionless figure.

"And if he hadn't twisted that foot around without noticing it, that's just what I'd have done!" he muttered, hunkering lower in the brush.

For long minutes he crouched without sound or motion, listening for the slightest indication of the presence of the killer. He heard nothing, saw nothing. Overhead birds chirped and fluttered. A small rodent scampered past, evincing no alarm. Gradually Hatfield became convinced that there was nothing in human form near him. He eased out of his cramping crouch and slowly and carefully began searching the surrounding terrain. After a period of meticulous examination of his immediate surroundings he was positive that the slope contained no life other than its legitimate feathered and four-footed denizens. He worked back to where he could again get a view of the dummy behind the ledge. Some instinct warned him not to approach it. He could not divine what danger could rest in the bundle of straw and old clothes, but just the same an urgent sixth sense told him to let the apparently harmless creation strictly alone. Finally he retraced his steps to where he had left Goldy. Mounting he rode boldly up the slope and back to the ledge. Again he studied the lifelike form. He dismounted, slipped his sixty-foot rope free and worked up the sag as far as was practicable. He built a tight loop and snaked it underhand toward the dummy. It was a difficult cast, with twigs and branches in the way, but at the third try he dropped the loop over the dummy's head and shoulders. Taking up the slack he jerked sharply on the rope.

There was a blaze of yellowish flame, a bursting ball of smoke and a terrific crash. Hatfield was hurled backward by the concussion. Half stunned he picked himself up, spoke a quieting word to his snorting horse, and stared toward the ledge.

Where the dummy had rested was a sizeable hole in the ground, with smoke still wisping from it. The dummy had disappeared and the ledge was cracked and shattered.

Hatfield drew a deep breath. The narrowness of his escape from death or a horrible mangling had shaken him not a little.

"I see it all now — marvel of perspicacity —" he muttered. "The hellion deliberately allowed me to spot him from down below, figuring I'd come looking for him, as I did. Had his trap all ready for me. When he was sure I'd fallen for his lure he rode on about his business, leaving the chore of picking up what was left of me to the buzzards. Looks like I'm up against a real, nice, gentle variety of hydrophobia skunk."

With a last glance at the ominous crater, which he had no desire to investigate more closely, he forked the sorrel and rode back to the camp in a very sober frame of mind.

Wallace, and every other living thing within several miles, heard the explosion. He excitedly asked Hatfield if he knew what had caused it. Hatfield told him, in terse sentences. Wallace's face went white.

"Is there no limit to what they'll do?" he muttered thickly.

"Looks like there isn't," Hatfield admitted. "And no limit to somebody's ingenuity. That was a brand of drygulching I never encountered before. Calculated to be even more effective than the standard variety, and safer for the drygulcher. Well, the chances are we've heard the last from him in that particular line, anyhow. When he learns his cute little scheme backfired, as it were, I figure he'll give the camp a wide berth. Have to look for him to bust loose someplace else."

"Hatfield," Wallace asked, "have you any notion who it is?"

"Yes," the Ranger said slowly, "yes, I've a notion, but it seems so darn absurd I'd rather not talk about it — yet."

"And if things keep going like they have been, very likely you won't get a chance to talk about it later, at least not in this world," Wallace predicted pessimistically.

CHAPTER 10

Two days later, on a bright and sunny afternoon, Hatfield rode up the gentle north
slope toward the rim of the cup. A little distance below the crest he dismounted, loosened Goldy's cinches, removed the bit and
turned him loose in a little grassy clearing
where a spring bubbled from under a rock.

"You just take it easy for a spell," he told
the sorrel. "I'm going to mosey on up and
work around to the top of those south
cliffs. Want a little look-see at things from
up there. Maybe there's something interesting that can't be spotted from down
below."

It was not too difficult to follow the rim
of the cup on the west side, although there
were spots that were a bit ticklish. Finally,
without mishap, Hatfield reached the crest
of the rock wall directly above the agitated
pool where the overflow of the spring dived
into the ground. From this point of vantage he studied the cliff over the spring,
against which the sunlight beat strongly.

In the fierce glare it showed seamed and

broken and fissured. From these and other indications he decided there had been a settling of the shattered strata over a period of many years. Doubtless the opening through which the big stream of water gushed forth had formerly been much larger.

His eyes grew thoughtful as he studied the peculiarly ribbed and striated surface, his tall form outlined in the blaze of the sunlight.

"Looks like a few good licks with a sledgehammer would knock those rocks down," he mused. "And if they did slip down, they'd block the spring completely. I've a notion just a little jar would cause the whole fault to collapse. That thing will need a bit of watching."

Still gazing at the jagged wall, he fished out the makin's and started to roll a cigarette. A sudden gust of wind flipped the paper from between his fingers. It fluttered to the ground and slithered toward the lip of the cliff.

Hatfield stopped quickly to retrieve it, and a bullet yelled through the space his body had occupied the instant before. And even as he heard the crack of the rifle far up the western slope, a second slug grazed his forehead.

Although the contact was slight, hardly enough to draw blood, the shock was terrific. He reeled, staggered, lost his balance and fell over the lip of the cliff.

As he rushed downward toward the surface of the pool, by a convulsive writhe and twist he managed to straighten his body and strike water feet first. He had but time to draw one quick breath, filling his lungs to the utmost, before he was sucked down into the cruel, swirling blue depths.

Down and down and down he rushed, powerless against the irresistible might of the vortex. It was senseless to struggle, to try to swim, to do anything but hold his breath and wonder if his frightful downward progress would ever be stayed.

It was, with a bewilderingly abrupt change of direction. He shot forward at amazing speed, still utterly helpless in the terror that gripped him. The terrific force of the compressed water threatened to crush his bones, his temples pounded, the blood roared in his ears, there seemed to be a white-hot band tightening and tightening about his chest, and he felt he could not hold his breath a second longer.

Then with the same uncanny suddenness he broke surface. He had barely time to release the stale air from his tortured lungs and gulp in another breath before he went under again. This time, however, he did not remain submerged for so long. He managed to cough up some of the water he had swallowed, pump some air in and out and get his movements a bit under control. But he still rushed onward through the stygian blackness with the air quivering to the roaring and rumbling of the swift water.

Gradually, however, the sound lessened a little, an indication that there was more room for the echoes to disperse, and as the uproar dulled, the onward rush of the stream slackened, slowly at first, then swiftly.

Weighed down by his clothing and his guns, Hatfield began to have trouble keeping his head above water, and still it was impossible to swim against the current. His arms were heavy as lead, his body beginning to numb, despair to grip his mind. It was becoming more and more apparent that he was doomed to a watery grave here in the echoing blackness.

Everything in this tunnel of infernos seemed to happen abruptly. The shallowing of the stream was in accord with other developments. One moment he was stroking against swift, deep water, the next the toes of his boots dragged over a pebbly bottom and the current was negligible.

The explanation, of course, was a sudden broadening of the devilish underground river. Hatfield didn't waste time pondering it. He struggled and splashed himself to his feet and began reeling sideways across the stream. His boots struck dry ground, slogged over it a few steps. Then he butted into a rock wall, hard. He sagged against it, clutching the rough surface, and rested for a couple of minutes. He batted his hands together until they were fairly dry, wiped his face and batted them some more.

He had matches in a tightly corked bottle which, fortunately, his tumble from the cliff and the battle with the current hadn't broken. He carefully uncorked the bottle and fished one out. The rock wall was dry and when he scraped the head of the match against it he got a light.

The tiny flame almost blinded him after the black darkness, but before the match burned out he saw he was in a rock walled and ceiled tunnel perhaps eight feet high by twice that in width. On the far side, the water washed the wall, but where he stood was a little strip of pebbly beach that stretched a couple of yards from the wall to the stream.

"Well, I know where I am," he muttered. "I'm right here, and darned lucky to be here, too. An inch to the right for that slug and I wouldn't be. And if that funnel mouth through which the spring empties had been a few yards longer I still wouldn't be here. The big question now is where to go?"

The answer was comparatively simple. He couldn't go back the way he came. The only thing was to follow the underground stream. It had to go somewhere, and his principle chore was to manage to stay alive till he got there. That is, unless the stream kept winding away inside the earth till it dried up.

However, being familiar with the peculiarities of the vast and shallow underground water system of this part of Texas, he felt that contingency was unlikely. More disquieting was the chance that the stream meandered in a tortuous route for so long that he would die of exhaustion and hunger before reaching some place where it might possibly emerge.

But be that as it might, he had no choice. His strength had returned and there was no use wasting time with conjecture. He set out downstream, keeping close to the wall with one hand brushing it to warn him of any change in direction. He stepped out briskly, feeling the need of exercise to drive the chill from his bones; the tunnel was not really cold, but cool enough to make his wet clothes unpleasantly clammy. As he trudged on with nothing untoward happening, his spirits rose. He'd already passed through so much unscathed he began to have confidence that the future was not as dark as it looked here in this home of blackness.

Nevertheless the strain on the nerves was great. It was a weird position to be placed in, trudging along through the bowels of the earth with only the whisper and ripple of the stream for company. The darkness was so impenetrable as to give an illusion of solidity. He could almost feel it press against his face, a yielding, billowy softness that opened up to allow him to pass and then instantly closed in behind him.

As the stream scrambled along for hour after hour and his weariness increased, his spirits ebbed. It began to look like he would never come to the end of this strange burrow inside the earth. He wondered how many untold ages it had taken the action of the water to eat this seemingly endless corridor through the eternal rock. There was comforting evidence that once upon a time a much greater volume had poured through the lightless drain. Such a torrent would surely have burst out somewhere. But where? The monotony of invisible stone stretched on and on. Hatfield knew he must have already covered many miles. He had not the slightest idea in which direction he was travelling, the twists and turns of the tunnel were many and confusing, but it apparently maintained a fairly uniform height and width. At times he sloshed through a film of water, but sooner or later the little strip of beach resumed.

The first indication that he might be nearing some opening was an acceleration of the flow of water. Soon it was fairly hissing past the rock wall on the far side of the stream, and Hatfield realized the gentle slope of the ground had changed to one of considerable steepness.

This brought a new and disturbing apprehension. He might be approaching a fall of some height. He strained his ears for the first ominous rumble that would bespeak plunging water.

None came, although the descent grew steeper and steeper. Now the rushing water was filling the tunnel with sound. The cheerful purring had become an angry mutter. And the tunnel floor, which had been surprisingly smooth, was ridged and rough, with a littering of loose stones that made walking difficult.

Hatfield struggled on. He was too deathly weary for anything to matter much anymore. He stumbled over the stones in a dogged, hopeless fashion. Once he fell, and lay for a long time before the subconscious urge to save his life finally brought him to his feet again to reel and stagger drunkenly over the uneven terrain.

Abruptly he realized he was walking in water that steadily grew deeper. It rose to his ankles, his knees, tugging at his legs, increasing the difficulties. His gait slowed to a sloshing shamble and it was more instinct than anything else that caused him to slow more and more as the pull of the current grew steadily fiercer. He groped along the stone wall in an aimless sort of way and it was a feeling of mild surprise more than anything else that he experienced when the hand questing out in front of him touched solid rock that barred his way.

He halted, pondering the matter in an abstract manner. He was barred from further progress, that was apparent, but the stream was still going some where, and one corner of his numbed brain, a little more active than the rest, insisted that he and the stream were taking this trip together. He struck a light to see what had stopped him and didn't stop the stream. He fumbled a match from the bottle and struck it on the wall. The dazzling flicker of light jolted some of the cobwebs from his brain and at the same time revealed an abrupt lowering of the roof. The stream passed under it, running swiftly, with perhaps eighteen inches to spare. He stared stupidly at the narrow opening above the water until the match flame burned his fingers. The quick sting of fire roused him a little more from the numbing lethargy of utter fatigue and hopelessness. He struck another match and studied the situation a bit more logically.

There was but one thing to do — trust himself to the water again. The quickening current hinted at rapids or a fall not far ahead, but he had little choice. No choice, in fact. The only alternative to risking the rushing water was to die of exhaustion or starvation. A swift death was preferable.

And then he suddenly realized something that sent a surge of hope through his being, quickened the beat of his heart and cleared his mind. A strong current of air was pouring from the opening; he could feel it fanning his face. And — air draws inward, not outward!

The only answer could be an opening somewhere ahead, and judging from the strength of the air current, no great distance off.

Hatfield drew a deep breath, tightened his belt, debated for a moment whether to discard his guns and boots, and decided not to. The current would buoy him up and if there was no obstacle ahead, he would very likely not be in the water for long. If there was a bad fall, well, he'd be dead in a few minutes. He waded to the middle of the stream. The current lifted him off his feet and he shot beneath the dense arch of rock that hung less than two feet above the surface of the rushing water.

On he sped, faster and faster. The water was roaring now and tossing and heaving. He had difficulty keeping his face above the surface. The blackness remained unrelieved by any ray of light and to his ears came an ominous rumbling sound. Undoubtedly he was approaching a fall. He drew a deep breath and grimly awaited the end.

Without the slightest warning he was enveloped in a blaze of radiance. He was outside the tunnel, and it was night; but in contrast to the hours of utter darkness he had undergone, the faint shimmer was as the glare of noonday and almost blinded him. Before he could shake his scattered senses together, he was swept over a smooth, curving lip and plunged downward.

Down he plummeted, the water pounding him with tons of weight, blinded, choked by spray. Then with a sullen plunge he struck the catch basin at the foot of the fall, which, after all, was of no great height. Again half drowned, he fought his way from beneath the crushing liquid hammers, struggling and floundering to at last scramble onto firm ground and lay gasping and retching. He hadn't the slightest idea where he was, and he didn't care. He was out of that horrible hole and that was enough for the moment.

Gradually his strength returned somewhat and he began to shiver with cold. He got stiffly to his feet and gazed about. So far as he could make out he was at the bottom of a shallow canyon. The stream, which was chuckling and purring again, as if it also were thankful to be free of the realms of darkness, had wooded banks, the growth evidently extending up the slopes, one of which began nearby.

Walking with difficulty, he pushed his way into the chaparral and began raking dry leaves together. When he had collected a sizeable pile he touched a match to it, feeding the flames with twigs and dry branches till he had a roaring blaze. With considerable difficulty he managed to tug off his boots and empty them. Next he removed his clothes, wrung the water from them and spread them close to the blaze. He rubbed his body to a glow and proceeded to thoroughly thaw out. He was a mass of bruises and ached in every joint and muscle. Otherwise he was apparently little the worse from his hazardous adventure.

Holding his garments to the blaze he dried them after a fashion and donned them again. Then he built up the fire and collected more leaves for a bed. Blind with weariness, he stretched out beside the blaze and was almost instantly asleep.

CHAPTER 11

The sun was shining brightly and birds were singing in the thickets when Hatfield awoke. For some minutes he lay drowsily thinking that it was a miracle that he was alive.

"Through no fault of my own, though," he told himself. "I climb up top that infernal cliff and make myself a perfect target for that hellion who'd evidently holed up on the slope again, watching my every move. If I hadn't dropped the cigarette paper at just the right second he'd have drilled me dead center. Then I had to pick just the right place to tumble off the cliff, with the water beneath me instead of hard rock. Why I didn't drown, I'm darned if I know. And the breaks kept coming my way and I found a hole to crawl out of the ground. Guess my number just wasn't up. But if I don't start using my head for something else besides holding up a hat, it will be up, and soon. So far I've been outsmarted at every turn. At this rate, Captain Bill will have to come over and snake me out of the mess. Oh, well, it's a long worm that has no turning, and anyhow, I'm getting a notion about a gent. Maybe if I can manage to stay alive a while longer, I'll get a mite more than a notion."

He got to his feet, wincing with the pain the effort entailed. He felt as if he'd been dragged through a knothole and hung on a barbed wire fence to dry. However, aside from some stiffness and soreness, everything appeared to be in working order. He left the thicket and took stock of his surroundings.

He was at the bottom of a canyon, all right, the near slope of which rose, not too steeply, to a rounded crest something over a thousand yards above. Doubtless from the crest he could get a view of the surrounding country. Without more delay he began to climb.

As he made his way up the slope his muscles limbered and by the time he reached the top he was in pretty good shape again. From the point of vantage he could see that, as he surmised, he had passed right through the belt of hills north and east of Cameron and was near their southern terminus. To the east was rangeland which was doubtless part of Bull Radcliff's holding. He decided the lumber camp must be north by west and some ten miles distant.

Not a pleasant prospect, a ten-mile trudge in his high-heeled boots, but there was no help for it. He descended to the level ground and headed north.

He had covered some three miles when he saw a rider on a big roan horse approaching from the north.

"May be a chance for a lift," he told himself hopefully. "That is, if it isn't some jigger with notions."

Against this contingency he loosened his guns in their sheaths and walked on. The rider had evidently sighted him and was veering in his direction. A few minutes later he saw it was a girl, and as she drew still nearer he recognized the girl of the Cameron station platform, Bull Radcliff's daughter Helen. Another couple of minutes and she reined in beside him.

"For heavens' sake!" she exclaimed. "What are you doing out here on foot?"

"Just taking a stroll before breakfast," he replied easily.

She stared at him as if convinced she was holding converse with a lunatic. A not unreasonable assumption under the circumstances, he was forced to admit.

"Why, I know you," she said. "You're

Mr. Jim Hatfield, Cl— Mr. Wallace's logging foreman. I remember seeing you that day on the station platform, when he saved me from falling flat on my face."

"Are you sure?" Hatfield countered, his eyes dancing.

"Sure of what?"

"That you didn't fall flat on your face?"

She stared again, then she got the implication and colored prettily.

"He — he talked a lot about you," she added hurriedly and with considerable confusion of manner. "He thinks you're wonderful.

"But never mind," she continued, "you still haven't told me what you're doing way out here on the range in such a condition. You look as if you'd been caught in a bad rainstorm, and your face is all bruised."

Hatfield decided that she had an explanation coming, and that the truth would serve best. In a few terse sentences he told her.

"And you came all this way under the ground!" she marvelled. "Why, it's a miracle!"

"Not so much so as it appears at first glance," he answered. "This part of the country is a web of underground streams. A creek will flow along on top of the ground for a long ways, then suddenly dive into a hole and reappear again miles distant. It's a limestone region, and a limestone strata is always honeycombed with caves and tunnels. I got into one and just had to keep on walking till I found a hole to crawl out of, that's all."

"I still think it's a miracle," she said. She shuddered. "And you say somebody tried to kill you?"

"Well, I don't think he was shooting just to scare," Hatfield returned grimly.

"I don't know what the country's coming to," she said, her red lips trembling. "Such terrible things have been happening. And I can't understand what's got into people all of a sudden. My father used to have hosts of friends. Everybody liked him and he liked everybody. Now it seems everybody hates him and he hates everybody in turn. Why do men have to be like that?"

"I don't know," Hatfield admitted soberly, and added, "but I've a notion it will all straighten out before long."

"I hope so," she sighed. "But here I am talking your ear off, just like a woman, and you must be dead on your feet and starved to boot. I've got to get you back to camp, somehow. I don't know whether this horse will carry double, although goodness knows he's strong enough."

"Suppose I fork him and pack you in front of me," Hatfield suggested.

"That might work," she conceded. "We'll try it."

She slipped lithely to the ground. Hatfield mounted the big roan, reached down, lifted her lightly and cradled her against his breast. The horse looked a little astonished but, recognizing a master hand on his bridle, offered no objection.

"Comfortable?" Hatfield asked as he turned the horse and headed him north.

"Quite," she replied, "but I'm afraid it's a terrible strain on your arms."

"I'll bear up under the strain," he chuckled. "A pity it's only a few miles to camp."

Her wide eyes regarded him thoughtfully. "I wonder," she said, "do you always affect people as you do me?"

"How's that?" he asked.

"Make them feel that they've known you a long time instead of just a few minutes."

"The boring are apt to create such an impression," he replied.

"You don't believe it and you don't mean it," she said. "And I'm beginning to understand why Clark Wallace raves about you so."

"Why?"

"Because," she said slowly, "you instill a feeling of security."

"Thank you," he said simply.

"Yes, that's it," she said. "A little while ago with just a few words you dispelled my fears for the future and made me believe that things really will straighten out before long."

"Keep on believing it, little lady," he said softly. "Just keep on believing it hard enough and it'll come true."

They rode on in silence. Presently Helen remarked, "We're pretty close to our ranchhouse, now; it's just the other side of that long ridge."

"And if your dad happens to see us, the chances are I'll learn if I can outrun buckshot," Hatfield predicted.

"Don't worry," she replied. "Dad's bark is a lot worse than his bite. He told me about the run-in he had with you and how you handled him, and he grinned while he was telling it. He said, 'If I was just twenty years younger, I'd take that young squirt apart and find out what makes him tick, but as it is, I reckon I'll have to leave him in one piece!' Then we both laughed. To tell the truth, I've a wee bit of a notion that he likes you."

Helen pointed to a narrow trail winding through the timberland on their left. "That will take us to the Coronado north of dad's cutting," she said.

They entered the forest track and rode through the beautiful woods and under the scarlet and amber arches of the fading oaks.

"A mighty pretty country," Hatfield said. "Wide and clean, and big enough for all. Ready and waiting to hand out peace and prosperity and happiness and content. You'd think, with such a garden spot to live in, that men's minds would turn to peace, brotherhood, and good will toward one another.

"But that day's coming," he added with conviction. "Present conditions are only temporary, the backwash. It's just like the tide rolling in from the sea. It comes forward and it recedes, then comes again, and each time just a little farther; and each time when it recedes it leaves a wider stretch of sparkling, clean-washed beach. That's the way it'll be here. Yes, the day's coming."

"And you'll help to make it come," she said softly, raising her piquant little face to gaze into his eyes.

CHAPTER 12

The most astonished man in Texas was Clark Wallace when Hatfield rode up to the camp with Helen in his arms. He stared, gasped, goggled, then began sputtering questions.

"Never mind the questions now," Helen told him as she slipped to the ground. "He's worn out and starved. Let him rest and get him something to eat. Don't stand there gaping! Do as I tell you!"

Hatfield chuckled under his breath as the stupefied Wallace obeyed.

"Son, I've a prime notion as to who's going to be the boss of the family," he said to Clark Wallace. "Begins to look to me like she took after Bull Radcliff a mite, after all."

While he ate everything placed before him, Hatfield gave Wallace an account of his misadventure.

"And now," Hatfield said as he pushed back his plate and lit a cigarette, "if you'll tell a wrangler to get the rig on a horse for me, I'll ride up and get my own cayuse. He must be feeling mighty put out about now."

"Why can't I do it?" Wallace asked. "You must be worn out."

"I'm okay," Hatfield replied. "I had a good sleep and this first class surrounding has put me back in shape. I'd like to sort of look things over up there, anyhow."

"But for heaven's sake don't go prowling around on top of that cliff again," pleaded Helen.

"Don't imagine there'd be any risk," Hatfield answered. "The chances are the jigger who threw the lead at me figured I was done for. Sure must have looked that way. For a while I wasn't so sure but what I was, myself. You stay here and look after the lady, Clark."

In the thicket on the north slope, Hatfield found a very disgusted Goldy who otherwise was none the worse. He transferred to the big sorrel and rode to the rim of the pool, pausing just above where the spring gushed from the rock wall beneath. For some time he studied the terrain, his eyes thoughtful.

"Wonder if that sidewinder just had cashing me in in mind, or was he anxious for me not to learn something?" he mused. "Be that as it may, I'm beginning to get a notion how it would be possible to put Wallace's flume out of business for good. Wonder if somebody else has hit on the same thing? Something to think about, anyway. And I think it wouldn't be a bad idea to post a guard up here below the rim, day and night."

Still very thoughtful he rode back to the camp. Wallace was not there when he arrived, having selected to ride part of the way home with Helen. Hatfield lay down for a couple of hours, then, after more cups of coffee, he got the rig on Goldy and headed for town.

Arriving at Cameron, he went at once to the Greasy Sack. The first thing he saw when he entered the saloon was Bull Radcliff and Chuck Hooley sitting at a nearby table enjoying a meal.

Radcliff glanced up, hesitated, as if half inclined to speak, apparently changed his mind and turned back to his dinner. Hooley scowled at the Lone Wolf and went on eating.

Hatfield walked to the bar, ordered a drink and rolled a cigarette.

"Well, unless Chuck Hooley is just about the best actor that ever stepped on the boards, he's out of the picture," he told himself. "When a jigger figures sure for

135

certain he's cashed in a hombre and then sees that same hombre walking in the door, he's pretty likely to register a little emotion of some kind. Hooley didn't bat an eyelash and just looked as if he'd like to punch me in the nose if he thought he could get away with it. Now where the devil do I stand?"

Again a vague notion filtered through his mind; but it seemed so darned preposterous to think that Alton Lee, the reputable contractor and engineer, was the answer. And yet, of all his possible suspects, Lee was the one man he had encountered who appeared to possess all the qualifications to fit into the picture. Lee, a highly certificated engineer, undoubtedly would have the knowledge of geology and petrology necessary to spotting the peculiar fault in the cliffs that walled in the natural reservoir and to comprehend its possibilities. There was no doubt but that Lee was a cold proposition. And he stood to profit greatly if the T & W won the race to Alpine Pass. Also, Lee would know how to use explosives.

"It doesn't seem to make sense, but there it is!" he muttered. "Oh, the devil! I just seem to be running around in circles!"

He considered the T & W crowd. That the financiers and operators back of the railroad were good at cutting corners and making questionable deals was common knowledge. They were a rather ruthless bunch, with an eye always out for a quick profit and with scant consideration for the welfare of others. But there was a limit. It seemed ridiculous to think that any high official of the great corporation would resort to murder to obtain an objective, but with millions at stake, you never could tell.

Sipping his drink, he pondered the amazing importance of little things. The displacement of a few rocks might spell success or failure of the vast C & P project. A few rocks, a few drops of water.

Hatfield had not altogether ruled out Bull Radcliff and Chuck Hooley. The conversation between Radcliff and Alton Lee stuck in his mind. Radcliff had rather broadly intimated that he was prepared to go to any lengths to defeat the C & P in the race for Alpine Pass. Radcliff did not strike him as the sort that would skulk in the bushes and wait for a chance to shoot a man down in cold blood. Bull Radcliff was undoubtedly a good hater, and hate encourages the very worst in a man's nature to take over, and if allowed to become a ruling passion, often the worst does become dominant. Such might well be the case with Radcliff.

Chuck Hooley, Hatfield felt, was capable of anything. All that he had been able to learn concerning the man corroborated that deduction. And if Hooley were really guilty of the drygulching, there was possibly a logical explanation of his lack of surprise at Hatfield's appearance. Perhaps someone had seen him riding with Helen Radcliff and had relayed the word to Hooley. Then the logging boss would have known that the apparently successful attempt on Hatfield's life had failed. If that happened to be the case, he naturally wouldn't show any surprise when he, Hatfield, walked into the saloon. All supposition, of course, but not to be overlooked.

Before Hatfield finished his drink, Radcliff and Hooley left the saloon together without a glance in his direction. Hatfield thoughtfully smoked a cigarette and he too left the Greasy Sack. He had decided to spend the night in town. He stabled Goldy and went upstairs to bed. He felt he needed a good night's rest and proceeded to get it.

After breakfast the following morning he repaired to the railroad station and requested an interview with Branch Bascomb, the C & P division superintendent. The super greeted him warmly but a bit apprehensively.

"Hope you're not dropping in to tell me you're having trouble at the logging camp," he said. "I've got enough on my hands without that."

"Everything going smoothly," Hatfield reported. "Trees coming down, the rams functioning perfectly, logs dropping down to the sawmill and the mill's booming."

"Well, I'm glad to get good news from somewhere," said Bascomb in tones of relief.

"What's the matter?" Hatfield asked. "You sound like the frazzled end of a misspent life."

"And that's just the way I feel," growled Bascomb. "Another infernal explosion over in the cut just this side of the bridge. Nobody hurt, thank God, but more men have quit because of it. If this keeps up we won't have enough workers left to spike a crosstie. I've been in touch with Mr. Dunn by telegraph all morning. He's over at the capital and he's sending men to replace those who quit. But if the situation doesn't change, it'll do no good. They'll quit, too. I wouldn't be surprised if Mr. Dunn himself comes over here. He had planned to return to Chicago today but the last wire I got from him said he was staying over till tomorrow at least, perhaps longer."

Hatfield nodded thoughtfully and was silent for a moment.

"I think I'll ride over to the bridge," he announced. "Would sort of like to have a look-see there."

"Okay, maybe you can find out something," grumbled the super. "You seem to be pretty good at trouble shooting. I'll give you a pass that'll get you by the guards. We've doubled the patrol since the last trouble. Not that it's likely to do any good," he added pessimistically. "Whoever sets that dynamite appears to be able to come and go as if he was a disembodied spirit. If I believed in ghosts I'd be inclined to think so."

"I've a notion the hellion is made of solid substance," Hatfield answered. "He's just been outsmarting everybody so far, that's all. Thanks for the pass. Chances are I won't leave the trail, but it's good to have if I should take a notion to."

As Hatfield rode through the defile, the guards patrolling the tracks eyed him watchfully; but he was riding an open trail and their authority did not extend beyond the right-of-way, so they made no attempt

140

to stop him. Some recognized him as Wallace's logging boss and called greetings.

Finally he reached a point not far from the bridgehead, where the cut had already been widened to accommodate the two main tracks and several sidings. Here was a scene of busy activity as the shovels and drills worked to widen the cut still more. A switch engine was shunting cars of material from the main line to the sidings, sorting them out for convenient disposal.

Hatfield pulled Goldy to a halt, rolled a cigarette and sat watching the busy scene. His keen gaze roved over every inch of the right-of-way in search of anything that might appear unusual, for he knew that it was near here that the last explosion had occurred.

The switch engine came puffing back almost to where Hatfield sat his horse, pulling a single car loaded with crossties. It screeched to a halt as the engineer applied the air. Hatfield saw him throw the reverse lever into forward position and reach for the throttle. A switchman swung a target from white to red, opening the siding switch. He turned and waved a fast "come-ahead" signal. A second switchman standing on the front step of the engine grasped the lever that would raise the coupling pin.

"Going to kick one down the siding," Hatfield told Goldy. "Watch her whizz!"

The locomotive's stack boomed, the drive wheels bit the rails, turned over faster and faster. The switchman on the step waved his hand up and down in the stop signal and jerked the lever, raising the pin and uncoupling the car from the engine.

The engineer slammed his throttle shut and applied the air. The engine came to a quick stop, but the car loaded with crossties, reeling and rocking, took the switch points and whizzed down the siding.

"You kicked that one too darn hard!" the conductor bawled peevishly to the engineer. "What you trying to do — knock a drawbar out?"

There was a string of cars already on the siding. The car of ties struck the rearmost with a crash of coupling draw-bars. The conductor opened his lips to shout further profane protest.

But what he said was never heard. It was drowned in a roaring explosion that seemed to cause even the adamant walls of the cut to rock and reel. Through a mushrooming cloud of yellow smoke Hatfield could see splintered crossties, portions of the car and earth and stone flying in all directions. Goldy gave a prodigious snort, rose on his hind legs and did a dance of pure terror. It was all Hatfield could do to keep him from wheeling and bolting back down the cut.

As the smoke cloud rose, Hatfield saw that pieces of the car and its load of ties were scattered all over the cut. The rails were twisted and broken. A hole in the ground showed where the car had stood. The engineer, dazed and bleeding, was picking himself up from the floor of the engine car. One switchman lay unconscious, the other was running about crazily, as if bereft of his senses.

The conductor was inanely bawling over and over again, "I told you you kicked it too darn hard! I told you you kicked it too darn hard!"

Hatfield realized that the chattering of the drills had ceased. The steam shovels swung idle. The cut rang with shouts and curses. Men were boiling toward the trail, completely demoralized, madly fleeing the scene of disaster. There would be no more work done this day.

Hatfield slipped from his horse and ran to the fallen switchman. A quick examination convinced him that the man was only stunned from the concussion and had not been struck by flying debris. Turning him over to the engineer, who had a cut on his forehead but was in full possession of his faculties, Hatfield went back to his horse and surveyed the scene of the explosion. The tie-loaded car had been blown to fragments, its load scattered far and wide. The nearest two cars of the string ahead lay on their sides, their loads spilled on the ground. In general, however, the damage done was comparatively slight.

The damage done to the morale of the workers, however, was anything but slight. They stood in tense groups, shaking their heads, pointing and grimacing, making no move to resume their work. The foremen did not attempt to get them back on the job. From the bridge beyond the cut, men were crawling down the web of superstructure like disturbed ants and hurrying to join their fellows in the cut.

A worried looking little man who turned out to be the construction engineer in charge of the project was dashing about asking questions.

"Another charge set under the rails," was the consensus of opinion, "but how in blazes did they do it?"

Hatfield hardly heard what was said. He

was gazing steadily at the shallow hole that marked where the car of crossties had stood on the rails. It was shallower, much shallower, than the one hollowed out by the explosion in Cameron, which undoubtedly took place beneath the locomotive.

"Feller," he told Goldy, "that one was not set off under the rails. The ground is hardly scratched. Whatever it was cut loose was in that car of crossties, not underneath it. Horse, I'm getting a notion. I don't know how the devil it was done, but I'm getting a notion about it."

He turned the sorrel and rode swiftly back to Cameron.

CHAPTER 13

When he reached town, Hatfield pulled up in front of the railroad station. He climbed the stairs to the offices on the second floor and sought out Superintendent Bascomb. In a few terse sentences he explained what had happened.

Bascomb swore luridly and paced the floor with nervous steps. Hatfield waited till he cooled down a bit and then remarked,

"I believe you said that Mr. Dunn is at the capital?"

"That's right," replied the super, "and I think I'll wire him to come over here and take charge. I'm licked!"

"You're not licked yet," Hatfield replied. "I want paper and a pencil."

The super motioned him to his desk. "Help yourself," he said. "Going to write an obituary for this project?"

Hatfield grinned, and used the pencil for a moment.

"Have that sent at once," he said, passing the paper to Bascomb.

The superintendent stared at the terse message, which was addressed to General Manager James G. Dunn and read:

I need a bit of authority over here.
(signed) Hatfield

"Why — who — what — how —" sputtered the super.

"I've known Mr. Dunn for years," Hatfield replied, and there was that in his voice that halted Bascomb's questions.

"Put a bug in the operator's ear," Hatfield added. "I know the rules forbid him to divulge the contents of a wire to anybody, but I want to be sure about this one. No slip-ups. You should get a hurry-up answer, unless they have trouble locating Mr. Dunn. I'm going over to the Greasy Sack for something to eat. I'll be there if you get the answer before I come back. If you do, send me word at once."

"Okay," Bascomb said resignedly. "I guess everybody's going loco so a little more lunacy on my part won't hurt. I'll have it sent at once."

Hatfield nodded and left the office. Before eating he stalled Goldy, gave him a rubdown and a good helping of oats.

"Liable to need you this evening, feller,"

he told the sorrel. "Take it easy!"

Hatfield was not particularly surprised when a messenger from Bascomb came hurrying in before he had finished his after-eating cigarette. He knew Jaggers Dunn wasn't given to wasting time. When he arrived at the office, the superintendent handed him the yellow telegraph form without a word. Hatfield nodded with satisfaction as he read:

To all employees of the C & P Railroad — Orders issued by James J. Hatfield are to be obeyed without question, implicitly, and at once. Superintendent Branch Bascomb will countersign this instruction.
(signed) James G. Dunn,
General Manager

"Let me have it and I'll put my signature on it," Bascomb said wearily. "After a while I suppose I'll wake up and see it's time to get out of bed."

"Well, anyhow you can rest assured you're not having a nightmare," Hatfield chuckled. "At least no worse than you've been undergoing recently while wide awake."

"Hatfield," the super pleaded, "can't you

148

give me at least a notion of what this is all about? Who the devil and what the devil are you that Jaggers Dunn will give you carte blanche to take over the whole blasted system?"

Hatfield chuckled again. Bascomb's bewilderment had its amusing side.

"I can't tell you everything right now," he replied. "As I said, I've known Mr. Dunn for quite a while and we've worked together a few times. What I hope and believe is that we're about to get to the bottom of what has been causing these mysterious explosions. I got a notion as I looked over the damage that one today did. But to put that notion into effect, I needed authority to give some orders and have them obeyed without question. Understand?"

"Oh, sure!" Bascomb said sarcastically. "It's all clear as a river full of mud."

Hatfield grinned at him and left the office.

The sun was setting in scarlet and gold when Hatfield rode out of Cameron. When he entered the defile, the kaleidoscope of color had faded to a monotone of dusty ash below and shadowy blue above pricked out with the silver needle points of the stars. He did not draw rein till he saw the shack, near the bridge-head, that he knew the chief construction engineer used for an office. A light burned within.

As he dismounted and approached the right-of-way, a member of the patrol halted him. However, the guard instantly honored Superintendent Bascomb's pass. Hatfield entered the office without knocking.

The engineer glanced up from his desk, considerably startled, as the Lone Wolf's tall form loomed in the doorway. Then he recognized his visitor.

"Why, hello!" he exclaimed. "It's Mr. Hatfield from Wallace's camp, is it not? You were pointed out to me today as you rode away from the scene of that infernal explosion. What can I do for you, Mr. Hatfield?"

Before replying, Hatfield drew up a chair and sat down.

"As I rode up the cut I noticed there are more than a dozen cars loaded with crossties on the siding," he said. "Well, I want those ties unloaded tonight, and spaced out on the ground so they can be given a thorough examination."

The engineer stared at him in slack-jawed amazement. "Oh, certainly, certainly!" he finally said, as one humors an imbecile. "But would you mind telling me

what you mean by making such a preposterous request?"

"You asked me what you could do for
me?" Hatfield reminded him with a smile.
Instantly, however, he became grave. "It's
nothing to joke about," he said. "I know it
sounds loco to you, but it's a deadly serious matter. Here's something I'd like you
to glance at."

He handed the engineer Jaggers Dunn's
telegram authenticated by the signature of
Superintendent Bascomb.

The engineer's bewildered astonishment
increased as he read the words. He raised
his eyes to Hatfield.

"Why — why I never experienced anything like this in my life!" he stuttered.

"And I reckon you've never experienced
anything similar to what you have on this
job of late," Hatfield returned grimly. Before the other could reply, he continued,
"I'm here, sir, by special request of General Manager Dunn to try and straighten
things out and to find out who's been
causing all the trouble in this section. I'll
admit I have little definite proof as to who
is responsible, but I do believe I've a notion how those explosions were set off. It's
just a hazy notion, but with good luck I
hope to find the answer tonight. Not only

does the hope of the C & P getting that bridge across the gorge and winning the race to Alpine Pass depend on the answer. Lives may depend on it as well. There's no time to waste. Get a gang together and start them unloading those cars. Get all the light you can — lanterns, torches, flares. Okay?"

"It's okay," the engineer agreed. "I don't know what it's all about, but anybody who works for Jaggers Dunn and doesn't obey his orders doesn't enjoy much peace of mind. I'll try and get a gang together over at the camp cars. The boys are pretty well demoralized after what happened today, coming on top of everything else, and I don't blame them."

"Promise them a full day at double pay, and tomorrow off," Hatfield directed.

The engineer nodded and led the way to the camp cars.

The workers had gotten over their scare and there was no trouble getting volunteers to unload the ties. They turned out and went to work. The ties were unloaded and laid in rows. Hatfield examined them with meticulous care. For several hours, results were barren. Then abruptly he uttered a satisfied exclamation. The tie before him was similar in appearance to the others.

But there was one marked difference: the wood was not live oak, but burr oak.

"I believe we've hit paydirt," he told the engineer. "Hold that light closer. Uh-huh, I thought so. Look at this, will you?"

The engineer peered at the almost unnoticeable opening in its surface some ten inches from the end of the tie. With the greatest care, Hatfield inserted the point of his knife and scratched. A gleam of metal rewarded his efforts.

"That's it," he said. "Just how it works I don't know yet, but we'll find out, if we last that long. I see the boys have finished with the last car of ties. Tell them to go back to their camp cars and stay there. Post a couple of your patrol guards to see the order is obeyed. I don't want anybody within a couple of hundred yards of your office."

The order was given. The wondering hands shuffled off through the darkness. Hatfield picked up the burr oak tie and shouldered it.

"I want you to get me some tools," he told the engineer. "A saw, a light hammer, a plane and a wood chisel will do."

While the construction man sought the tools, Hatfield carried the tie into the office and deposited it on the engineer's desk. He moved all available light close to the desk. By this time the other had returned with the needed tools. Hatfield took them and laid them on the desk beside the crosstie. Then he turned to his companion.

"Okay," he said. "Now you toddle along with the men. If something should go wrong, this whole shebang will be blown clean to Mexico."

The nervous little engineer swelled like a bantam rooster sensing a fight. He glared at Hatfield.

"You go to the devil!" he said.

Hatfield grinned, his eyes sunny. He patted the other on the shoulder.

"Good man!" he said. "Okay, we'll take our chances together."

Handling the tools gingerly, they went to work. Hatfield sawed off the end of the tie nearest the small aperture through which the gleam of metal could be seen, and found nothing. He tried again, a little farther along the oaken beam, with likewise barren results. A third attempt, however, an inch or so beyond the small hole, rewarded him with a sudden screech of the saw's teeth on metal. The engineer gasped and jumped.

"Getting hot," Hatfield remarked coolly.

"Somewhere between this and the far end we'll find it. Just about the middle, I'd say. Bring the light closer and let's make a try with the plane."

A few minutes of work and the rough outer surface of the tie was shaved off, revealing the reddish-white, close-grained wood. Hatfield laid the plane aside and closely examined the smooth surface.

"Look," he said to the engineer.

The latter, bending close, could clearly see a fine line of jointure that formed a rectangle in the surface of the wood cleared of the rough outer fibers.

Hatfield picked up the hammer and chisel. "Now comes the ticklish part," he remarked. "If I'm right, we'll find out how the darn thing works; if I'm wrong, well, I've a notion we'll find out a lot of things a bit sooner than we figured. Want to make a little bet who goes highest?"

"Oh, stop it!" snapped the other. "I'm about ready to have hysterics as it is. I don't believe you've got a nerve in your body!"

Hatfield chuckled. With a steady hand he fitted the sharp edge of the chisel against the hair-line jointure. The engineer went rigid as with a swift, sure stroke Hatfield drove the chisel into the tiny crack.

He held his breath and clenched his hands until his nails bit into his clammy, damp palms as Hatfield struck again and again, each time a little harder.

"That should do it," the Lone Wolf muttered. "So far, so good. Now let's see what happens when we tip it up. If it's a spring mechanism of some kind — curtains!"

He laid down the hammer and levered on the chisel, putting forth more and more of his strength. A section of wood rose slowly from the parent body of the tie. Higher and higher, until at one end an opening was revealed.

"Careful!" gasped the engineer. "I see something!"

"Uh-huh, the cap," Hatfield returned in unperturbed tones. "Reckon you can relax now. Nothing's liable to happen. It isn't a spring or a trembler, as I was afraid it might be. I think I'm beginning to understand the darned contraption."

He put more force on the chisel as he spoke. A moment later he seized the rectangle of wood and twisted it free, revealing a hollowed out section of the tie about a third of its length.

"And there's the charge," he said. "Three nice fat sticks of dynamite wrapped in felt to prevent a jar setting it off. Now let's see if we can figure how it works."

He examined the infernal machine carefully, his black brows drawing together.

"I got it!" he exclaimed. "Of all the devilish contraptions! Do you see it?"

"I'm — not sure," the engineer hesitated.

"Perfectly simple," Hatfield said. "Simple, but smart and devilish. Look, the tie was carefully hollowed out, so carefully that the slab of wood removed fitted back into place so nicely that the line of jointure was practically invisible. The capped dynamite was placed in the hollow, carefully wrapped to protect it from the jars incidental to handling the ties and spiking them into place."

"And the jar of the trains going over the rails finally set off the charge?" the engineer hazarded.

"Nope, not in the way you think," Hatfield replied. "That dynamite is so carefully protected that trains could roll over the ties till Judgment Day and not set it off."

"Then how —" the engineer began.

"The detonating contrivance is the real part of the darned thing," Hatfield interrupted. "See this steel pin that is so closely fitted into the hole bored in the tie. You'll notice the head of it comes almost to the surface. You see, too, that the pin is set at an angle and slightly curved. Now look close. See the point of the pin is almost touching the cap. Now notice where the hole was bored in the tie. So that the head of the pin comes exactly under the steel plate upon which the rail rests when it's spiked to the tie. Ties being of uniform length and being laid so that their ends are in line, it was easy to figure where the head of the pin should come. The tie plate would be almost touching the head of the pin. Begin to get it?"

"Sort of," the engineer admitted, mopping his sweating face with a handkerchief.

"I don't need to tell you," Hatfield resumed, "that as trains run over the rails, the weight pressing down on the rails tends to gradually force the tie plate into the wood of the tie. Old ties show that the plate has been forced down into the wood quite a ways. And in the case of those ties that blew up, as the plate sank deeper and deeper into the wood, it pressed the point of the pin against the cap. Each time a train passed over, the cap got a jolt. Finally the contact was so rigid that when a jolt came along, it jammed the point of the pin against the sensitive cap; it exploded and

158

set off the charge. That's all there is to it. Simple?"

"Simple!" snorted the engineer. "The man who rigged this up is a genius without a trace of conscience!"

"Uh-huh, a regular sidewinder with plenty of wrinkles on his horns," Hatfield agreed.

"It's a wonder one of the infernal things didn't go off while it was being spiked into place," the engineer observed.

"He thought of that and provided against it," Hatfield explained. "You'll notice that the charge is placed in the middle of the tie from each end, where no spike would be driven. And the pin is in the exact center between the two sides, where a spike wouldn't touch it except by some freak chance. Oh, he thought of everything! But he made one of the little slips the owlhoot brand always makes! He used burr oak ties instead of stealing some live oak ones."

As he spoke he gently lifted the charge from the hollow and laid it on the desk. With the greatest care, while the engineer again held his breath, he loosened the cap and set it aside. Then he replaced the slab of wood and tapped it into place.

"Put the sticks in the powder house and

keep the tie here in your office," he directed. "And here's your next chore. As soon as it is light, have every tie between here and Cameron examined. If you find one that's burr oak, snake it out, and snake it down carefully. First thing this morning I'll send down a crew of men who know wood from Wallace's camp. They'll help you look things over. I'll get in touch with Bascomb as soon as I get back to town and see to it that no trains are run west of Cameron until you give the word. And don't move your switch engines till you're sure it's safe to do so. Tell the men that we've cleared up the mystery of the explosions and that they won't have to worry about them any more. It'll be safe for them to go back to work. Reckon that takes care of everything. I'm riding to town."

The engineer hesitantly asked a question. "Do — do you know who is responsible for this outrage?"

"Not for sure," Hatfield replied grimly.

But although he did not care to say so, for he still had no proof, there was no longer much doubt in Hatfield's mind as to who was responsible. There was only one man in the section with the knowledge, brains, imagination and ability to rig up the lethal contrivance. That man was Alton Lee!

160

CHAPTER 14

The first rose of dawn was staining the eastern sky before Hatfield reached Cameron. He knew where Superintendent Bascomb slept and he did not hesitate to get him out of bed and give him a detailed account of the night's happenings.

Bascomb instantly had some things to say about Bull Radcliff but Hatfield brought him up short with the admonishment that there was no proof against Radcliff and that loose talking could easily do harm to a possibly innocent party.

"It's altogether too serious a matter for reckless accusations," he pointed out. "There's cold-blooded murder involved. There'll be enough talking as it is, without you giving it official sanction. Keep a tight latigo on your jaw till you know what you are talking about."

The division superintendent was not accustomed to being spoken to in so stern a manner, but he was forced to admit that what Hatfield said made sense. Suddenly he asked a question. "Hatfield, did Mr.

161

Dunn send you over here? Are you his personal representative?"

"Nope to both questions," Hatfield replied cheerfully. "He didn't send me, and I'm just his personal friend."

"There's something darned funny about all this," the super grumbled in injured tones. "I wish I knew who the devil, and what the devil you are!"

"Maybe you'll find out sometime," Hatfield smiled. "Chances are you will. At present I'm Clark Wallace's logging boss. That's enough for you."

"Oh, I suppose so," Bascomb admitted, "but I'm curious as an old maid who sees a man's shoe sticking out from under her bed. You have a way of making people jump when you crack the whip. I've a notion you'd even make Alton Lee jump, and nobody's ever been able to do that so far as I've noticed."

"What do you know about Alton Lee?" Hatfield asked.

"Oh, no more than most everybody else does, I reckon," Bascomb replied. "He's one of the smartest engineers that ever came down the pike, and he's a cold proposition. Knows all there is to know about the railroad business. He used to work for a railroad promotion outfit over East. There was a rumor, just a rumor, mind you, that the outfit was involved in some rather shady transactions. Political influence hushed up the matter, I understand, but Lee severed connections with them and went to work for the T & W. Can't say as he improved his associations much by doing so, although they always managed to stay inside the law. They're a bunch of predatory pirates, but so far as anybody knows they've never done anything that isn't legal. That's why I never took any stock in the talk that the T & W might be responsible for what's been going on here. In my opinion, they just don't play the game that way. They don't have to. They usually get what they want by slick conniving. In this particular deal, old man Dunn proved just a mite too smart for them. They planned to seize Alpine Pass and hold it till their line got there, but Dunn pulled a wire or two over at the capital and pointed out that an open trail runs through Alpine Pass, and you can't block off an open trail, not in Texas. So the Rangers told the T & W crowd to lay off, if they wanted the right-of-way through the Pass to get there first. That's when they gave the contract of pushing their road through to Alton Lee, figuring that if anybody could do it, he could; and if things don't get better for us in a hurry, he will. Despite the trouble he's been having with timber, his bridge is ahead of ours."

"I've a notion things will pick up for you, before long," Hatfield said, his eyes thoughtful.

"Hope you're right," replied Bascomb. "Anyhow, if what you figured out last night proves to be the right answer, I've a notion they will. At least we'll be able to keep men on the job. The defection of workers is getting to be a serious matter."

Having been assured that no material or work trains would move west until the line had been pronounced safe, Hatfield headed for the Greasy Sack and an early breakfast. Then he rode to the logging camp. When he arrived he immediately dispatched a crew to assist in inspecting the crossties. After making sure that everything was under control and running smoothly, he lay down and slept for several hours, to awake much refreshed.

"Where's Wallace?" Hatfield asked the cook as he was having a snack in the kitchen. "He wasn't around when I rode in this morning."

"Reckon he stayed overnight in town," the cook replied. "He rode away late yesterday evening, said he had to put in an order for some supplies."

Hatfield nodded. "Tell him I'll be over to the cutting if he shows up before I get back," he directed.

The formation where the stand of live oak grew was peculiar. To the west was open range, the line of demarcation between the growth and the grassland surprisingly regular. To the east was a rocky and barren ridge that sloped up steeply for more than a thousand yards. Shouldering this ridge on one side and the grassland on the other, the timber grew up the mountain for nearly two miles from where the cutting now stood. The face of the cutting extended from the treeless range to the base of the ridge.

At the edge of the cutting Hatfield paused to view the busy scene. Axes rang, saws rasped and the swishing and rumbling of falling trees added a deep undertone to the sharp mechanical sounds. As soon as the great trunks were topped and the branches cut away, chains were affixed to the logs and teams of horses snaked them along a road built for the purpose to where they would take the flume and be whisked down to the pool beside the sawmill.

Hatfield turned and gazed down the slope denuded of trees. He shook his head. It was a weird tangle of tree tops, branches and dry leaves. He gazed up the slope. The stand of oaks were a flame of the scarlet and gold of late autumn, with wide blotches of brown where the leaves were devoid of moisture and ready to fall. He turned back to the lower slope. More than once he had eyed the litter disapprovingly. Now he decided it was time to do something about it. He beckoned the team foreman who was supervising the chaining of a log.

"Rader," he said, "I don't like that mess down there."

"I don't like it either, sir," the foreman agreed, "but we've always been in such a hurry to get the stuff out that Mr. Wallace said we'd take a chance and leave it lay."

"Well, we're not taking a chance any longer," Hatfield replied. "Start your crew and your teams snaking the tops and branches here down the slope. I want a cleared space of at least a hundred yards extending downward from the edge of the cutting; and I want the tops and branches that are brought down during the day moved each evening. If a fire should start in that litter, very quickly a heat would be generated that would start a top fire in no time. The leaves on the trees are dry and the sap has almost ceased to rise. Such a top fire would sweep the whole stand to the mountain crest, sweep it clean, especially if a wind was blowing up from the south. A wind wouldn't be needed, for that matter. That ridge over there creates a natural draft that would grow fiercer by the minute as the heat increased. If conditions were ordinary, we might take a chance on leaving the stuff where it is, but a lot of funny things have been happening in this section of late. Somebody else might realize the potentials of that litter. I've a feeling we've just been lucky that somebody hasn't tumbled to it before."

"I think you're absolutely right," replied the foreman. "I saw a fire start in a mess like that over around Lake Tahoe in California. It destroyed thousands of acres of fine pine. Could happen here. I'll get busy right away."

Hatfield watched operations for a while; then, satisfied that everything was running smoothly, he returned to the camp. Soon afterward Clark Wallace rode up to the clearing in a great state of excitement.

"Everybody is talking about what you did last night," he told Hatfield. "The

167

town's all torn up and arguments going on in every direction. There was even some talk of lynching Bull Radcliff, but Sheriff McGregor put a stop to that. He said if anybody started a necktie party in his bailiwick there'd be some cases of lead poisoning, and he had his old ten-gauge shotgun loaded with blue whistlers to back it up."

Hatfield looked grave. He knew the situation was explosive. The men who had been killed by the planted dynamite had friends who didn't take kindly to their murder. He felt confident that McGregor could hold down any organized attempt to make trouble, but individual reactions were something else. A sudden flareup of tempers and there might be tragic results.

"I'm worried about Radcliff," Wallace resumed. "I understand he's becoming very bitter and feels that he's getting a raw deal. And he has the devil's own temper. No telling what might happen if somebody should brace him."

Hatfield smiled a little. " 'Pears you've sort of changed your way of thinking about Radcliff," he observed.

Wallace flushed. Then he faced the Lone Wolf squarely. "Yes, I have," he admitted. "And I'll tell you why. I just can't see how a man responsible for the things that have been done hereabouts could have a daughter like Helen Radcliff."

Hatfield chuckled, his green eyes dancing.

Nevertheless, Hatfield was also worried about Radcliff. If he was right about Alton Lee, and Bull was unjustly suspected, he must harbor a bitter resentment, and there was no telling to what lengths that resentment would carry him under provocation.

Wallace wandered off to look after some chores. Hatfield left the building and walked slowly up the flume to the cliff base. For long minutes he stood intently studying the cliff face, his attention focused on the point where the hole had been blown in the wall.

"The difference in the rock there is almost imperceptible," he mused. "Only a trained eye would notice it. Bull Radcliff couldn't see it with a spyglass, and from all I've gathered concerning Chuck Hooley, he couldn't either. That is unless he's keeping under cover the fact that he's a highly educated engineer who specialized in petrology. And I'd bet a hatful of pesos that he isn't. So where does that leave the situation? Narrows it down to one man. Still seems a bit ridiculous to suspect

Alton Lee of such doings, but who else? Somebody was able to spot that one vulnerable portion of the cliff. It isn't wide, either, the result of a slip, perhaps a million years back. In the course of some geologic upheaval a whole section of rock moved over this way, from the east, I'd say, and settled down on softer strata that was perhaps the cap rock of the underlying granite. Throughout the ages the softer strata was compressed and narrowed by the tremendous weight resting on it. Gradually erosion weathered down the surface and laid the cliff face bare. A trained petrologist can read that page in geologic change. Well, it's up to me to give Senor Lee careful attention."

From his pocket he took a carefully folded paper that revealed nothing more unusual than a cigarette butt. For some minutes he studied the tiny white cylinder with the browned edges, then folded it up and replaced it in a buttoned pocket.

"Not much," he mused, "but could mean a lot. A shaley band of rock, a surgeon's knot, and a bit of paper and tobacco. Not much, but maybe enough. We'll see."

CHAPTER 15

Two days later, Hatfield rode to Cameron. At the base of the denuded slope stretching up the mountain he reined in for a moment. From where he sat his horse the tangle of tops and branches appeared to stretch upward to the very edge of the uncut timber. Hatfield knew it wasn't so, but the ominous litter was disquieting. He experienced an uneasy feeling that perhaps the cleared space between the mass of tinder-dry debris and the standing trees was not wide enough. Reason told him it was, but just the same he decided to have it widened a bit. He visioned the terrific welter of flames sweeping up the slope if the mess should by chance or design catch fire. No telling what the frightful heat might accomplish. He could feel the steady draft sucking along the bare, sun-warmed wall of the ridge, although otherwise the air was perfectly still. With even a slight wind blowing from the south, that steady pressure of air would increase to gale proportions. He shook his head and rode south on the Coronado Trail.

When he arrived at Cameron, Hatfield found Superintendent Bascomb in high spirits.

"Things are humming, thanks to you," he told the Ranger. "The boys aren't scared any more and are working like beavers. They're sore as blazes at the T & W bunch and swear they'll beat 'em out or bust a leg in the attempt. And today we got another crew Mr. Dunn sent over. Our bridge is creeping up on the T & W's and if nothing goes wrong we'll be even with them before the week's out. If you fellows will just keep pouring us the timber I believe we'll come out on top. It all depends on your sending us the stuff."

"You'll get it," Hatfield promised.

Leaving the superintendent, Hatfield repaired to the sheriff's office. He found McGregor busy at his desk. He waved Hatfield to a chair.

"Take a load off your feet," he invited. "I'll be finished in a minute."

Hatfield sat and smoked while the sheriff's pen scratched away at the letter he was writing. Abruptly he laid aside the pen, fixed Hatfield with his frosty eyes and asked a most unexpected question. "How's Bill McDowell?"

Hatfield did not bat an eyelash. "About

172

as common, I reckon," he replied. "Rarin' and chargin'."

"Sort of interested in the old Pelican," the sheriff remarked. "Him and me rode together for the XT, before you were born, I reckon."

Hatfield rolled another cigarette. "When did you catch on?" he asked.

"Oh, I had a notion that first day on the station platform," the sheriff replied. "You know the Lone Wolf has considerable of a reputation, especially among peace officers. I'd never seen you before but I'd heard you described by folks who had. The yaller horse just about cinched things, and after I watched you operate for a spell there wasn't much doubt in my mind. I figured, though, I'd better keep a tight latigo on my jaw, seeing you weren't saying anything. But after what you did the other night, I decided I might be able to lend you a hand in case you might need one."

"You may have something there," Hatfield admitted.

"Learned anything?" McGregor asked.

"Not much, except that somebody should stretch rope," Hatfield admitted.

"You can say that twice," grunted the sheriff, adding with apparent irrelevance,

"Folks are saying some hard things about Bull Radcliff."

"They're saying them wrong," Hatfield instantly stated. "Radcliff has neither the brains nor the knowledge to maneuver what's been going on."

"I never thought Radcliff was the sort who'd shoot a man in the back," the sheriff observed.

"I doubt if he is," Hatfield agreed. "But if he did, he'd use a gun and not some sort of complicated device. That would be beyond his understanding."

"Then who?" asked the sheriff. "The T & W crowd?"

"I don't think it's a crowd at all," Hatfield said. "In my opinion everything that's been done is the work of one man."

"One man?"

"Yes. Everything that's happened could easily have been handled by a single individual, and there has been a sameness of method that bears up the contention. Has it struck you that practically everything has employed the use of explosives?"

The sheriff tugged his mustache. "As I told you, Chuck Hooley is a top-notch powder man," he observed, again with apparent irrelevance.

"But what I said of Radcliff also goes for

Hooley," Hatfield countered. "He hasn't the required brains or knowledge, either."

"Don't you suspect anybody?" asked McGregor.

"I don't care to make intimations I'm not prepared to support with proof," Hatfield replied. "Guess I'll just have to keep on digging, and sooner or later maybe I'll strike paydirt."

"Understand you've always been good at that, and I reckon you will this time, too, if you manage to stay alive long enough," grunted the sheriff.

Three nights later the mysterious marauder struck again, and where Hatfield suspected he might.

It was the watchman atop the cliffs, guarding the rams, who spotted the fire. The banging of his six-shooter aroused the camp. The loggers tumbled out in all stages of undress to stare, muttering and cursing, at the ominous glow flaring up the southern sky.

Hatfield and Wallace hurried through the straggle of growth flanking the clearing till they could get a view of the cutting. The whole lower slope was a seething inferno fanned to ever fiercer fury by a strong wind booming up from the south.

From the mad welter rose smoke and

gases that took fire as they floated upward and mingled together, forming a gigantic sheet of living light that bathed the landscape in a ruddy glare. Corruscating sparkles sailed upward, intermingling with flakes of fire like to the blown-out sails of a burning ship. And ever the torrent of flame rolled up the slope with the roar and thunder of a rushing river.

Hatfield and Wallace stood spellbound by the stupendous display of pyrotechnics that seemed more appropriate to the terrors of the Pit than to the earth, the fierce glow beating on their faces, their breath catching in the withering heat.

But they quickly realized it was not one on which they could afford to linger. The belt of chaparral that flanked the clearing was already afire. Pale flickers showed where falling embers were igniting the dry leaves.

"Come on," Hatfield said. "We've got to get busy or the whole camp'll go up in smoke."

"If you hadn't removed the debris from below the uncut stand we'd lose every stick clear to the mountain-top," Wallace chattered as they ran back to the clearing.

"Guess that was the general notion," Hatfield replied grimly. "I only hope the fire doesn't jump the open space. It's a lot worse than I anticipated. Well, there's nothing we can do about that. Our chore now is to save the camp buildings."

As soon as they reached the clearing, Hatfield issued terse orders.

"Get buckets, pans, anything that will hold water," he told the loggers. "Douse the roofs and drench down the walls. It'll be hotter'n the hinges of hell hereabouts in a little bit, and embers will be raining down. We musn't let it get the jump on us. Move! everybody! Haul out those ladders from under the storehouse and form a bucket brigade."

The loggers jumped. Soon containers of water dipped from the flume were being sloshed over roofs and walls. As Hatfield predicted, the heat quickly grew terrific, sparks and burning embers showered down. The dry chaparral roared and crackled as flame swept through it. Dense clouds of smoke swirled and eddied; the air was thick with falling ash; breathing became increasingly difficult.

At first the men dashed to and from the flume, but soon they slowed to a walk, then to a shamble. Heads were swimming, lungs bursting, and ever the enervating heat grew worse, sapping the strength, blinding the eyes. The great fire on the slope was thundering past the camp, now, and adding its billows of smoke and its fiery waves of superheated air.

"Once it gets above the tip of the ridge, things will be better," Hatfield panted to Wallace who was with him on the roof of the big bunkhouse.

"They better get that way fast," the lumberman gasped reply. "We can't take much more of this. Look! The stable roof is afire!"

It was, a flame flickering up where an ember had fallen, but a big container of water doused it. But the roofs were steaming, the water drying almost as quickly as it struck the blistered shingles, and the embers fell in fiery clouds.

Men fell, also, choking and retching, burying their faces in the hot dust, breathing deeply for a moment of the cooler air close to the ground and then staggering erect again to reel toward the flume. Hatfield was conscious of a queer singing in his ears, a red mist before his eyes. His movements were slow, jerky, his arms heavy as lead. He knew the signs were those of asphyxiation. The air was foul with smoke and ash and there was little oxygen left to breathe. But he doggedly threw bucket after bucket of water on the smoldering shingles.

Wallace collapsed, limp, helpless. His flaccid body began to slide gently down the slope of the roof. In the nick of time, Hatfield grasped his collar and stopped his progress to the ground thirty feet below. After a terrific struggle he managed to get the unconscious man to a ladder, down which he was passed by others in little better shape than himself. Hatfield shook his head to free his brain of the smoky cobwebs that wreathed about it and went back to the task of throwing water. He had ceased to act with reason or forethought. His movements were jerky, mechanical, like those of an ill-adjusted automaton. Dully he wondered if his hearing was failing. The roar of the fire was not nearly so loud. Then he dimly sensed that somebody on the ground below was shouting his name. He listened, vaguely pondering just why all the fuss. Then suddenly he realized that the air was appreciably cooler, that no more embers were falling. His head cleared a little and he understood what was being said.

"Come on down, Jim," somebody was bellowing. "Come on down, before you tumble off and bust your neck. Everything's under control. The fire's past the tip of the ridge."

Without giving much serious thought to the matter, nothing seemed worth bothering about unduly anymore, he shuffled along the slanting roof until he reached a ladder. Automatically he found the rungs with his feet and began the descent.

But now the physical torment of breathing had lessened. Strength was flowing back into his limbs. His head was clearing. By the time he reached the ground he was getting close to normal. Around him the loggers, burned and blackened, red-eyed and haggard were grinning wanly.

"We did it!" one croaked. "Everything's safe, but Boss, how did you stand it up on that roof all the time?"

"Darned if I know," Hatfield admitted. "Seems I just sort of got stuck there, like I was melted down and glued to the shingles."

The loggers croaked and cackled with what was evidently intended for laughter.

"Wonder if it jumped the cleared space up above?" Hatfield asked.

"Don't think so," said Wallace, who had regained consciousness and aside from looking rather sick and weak, appeared none the worse for his experience. "Maybe we can work around the tip of the ridge and see. Less brush up there, or was, and maybe the ground isn't too hot to walk on."

The weary fire fighters made their way through the still smoldering ash to a point from where they could see up the slope. The fire was still burning but was now only a pale reflection of its former fury. And by the light of the flames they could see the ordered ranks of the great live oaks standing firm and untouched.

"Jim, you saved us with that clearing," Wallace said, breathing a deep sigh of relief. "But if you hadn't thought of doing it, well . . ."

"And we're saved the chore of cleaning up the litter," Hatfield chuckled. " 'Pears even most of the stumps are burned out. All ready for grass to take over and make good grazing land. Let's go get some coffee and something to eat. Fire fighting makes me hungry."

"And everybody has today off, railroad bridge or no railroad bridge," declared Wallace. "And anybody who doesn't go to town and get drunk to celebrate will get fired!"

The blackened loggers croaked a cheer and trooped back to the camp.

"Well, it looks to me like the hellions have just about played their last trick," Wallace observed as they ate hugely and downed cup after cup of steaming coffee. "They can't very well burn a flume full of water, the rams are guarded, and so is the sawmill. So far as I can see, there's nothing vulnerable left."

But Hatfield wasn't so sure.

CHAPTER 16

The next evening, Hatfield dropped in on Superintendent Bascomb.

"Everything going fine," the super said. "Our bridge is neck and neck with theirs now and we're two-thirds of the way across the gorge. They tell me if it hadn't been for you, that fire would have swept the whole mountain clean. That sure was smart thinking on your part. Looks like you're always a jump ahead of the hellions."

"Yes, but looks are sometimes deceiving," Hatfield replied. "You can never tell which way a pickle is going to squirt from its skin. I expect he — they still have something up their sleeves besides arms. The only thing to do is try and anticipate the next move. And I've a feeling that if the next one is put over it'll be curtains."

"Darn it! Now you've got me worried," the super complained.

Hatfield chuckled. "Don't mean to sound like a prophet of doom," he said, "but when you're up against something really bad, it doesn't do any good to play ostrich. Perhaps nothing more will happen, and then perhaps it will. We can't afford to take any chances, that's all I mean."

"Now, how the devil are you going to take a chance or not take a chance when you don't know what to expect?" Bascomb demanded.

"The idea is not to overlook any weak spots, and not to be lulled into a sense of false security," Hatfield explained. "This business is just like handling a herd of cows. When the critters seem perfectly placid and content is the time to watch them, or before you know it you've got a stampede on your hands. Be on the lookout for something when, apparently, there's nothing to worry about and you may forestall trouble. For instance, be sure your bridge guards are on the job every minute of the day and night. A well placed charge of dynamite there and you're sunk."

"Dynamite!" growled Bascomb. " 'Pears everything off-color that happens has dynamite in one form or another mixed up in it."

"It's a handy tool," Hatfield agreed, "especially in the hands of a man who knows how to use it. Well, I'm going over to the Greasy Sack for a drink and a bite to eat."

"Saw Bull Radcliff and his logging

foreman leaving there a little while ago," Bascomb observed.

"That so?" Hatfield answered. "How is Radcliff?"

"I don't think he's very happy," Bascomb replied. "You know folks are sort of looking sideways at him, and he knows what they're thinking. Small wonder that they are, though, the things that have been happening lately."

"The American way is to judge a man innocent until he is proven guilty," Hatfield remarked pointedly.

Hatfield had about finished eating when the man of whom he had been thinking entered the saloon and glanced around. Hatfield nodded and Alton Lee nodded back. He walked over to the Ranger's table.

"Was looking for Radcliff," he said. "Seen him around?"

"I heard he left here a little while ago," Hatfield replied. "Take a load off your feet and have a drink, maybe he'll drop back in."

"Thanks, don't mind if I do," Lee accepted and sat down. He toyed with his drink and for once seemed in a mood for conversation.

"Radcliff has been giving me better stuff of late," he observed. "Good thing, too.

The race is getting tight. Good timber is the key to the situation, as you know without me telling you. We hope to win, but nobody will drop dead if we don't. Radcliff takes the matter very seriously, though, in my opinion more so than is warranted. After all, a business matter is not something to get so worked up about. I know he had a fearful row with his neighbors over the question of the railroad coming through this section and is out to even the score. But those old-timers don't like to be thwarted or have their opinions flouted. As they say out here, Radcliff has sure got his bristles up."

"Never can tell what a jigger will do when he's really pawing sod," Hatfield admitted.

Lee nodded and drew a flat leather case from his pocket. He snapped it open and selected a cigarette from its contents. Hatfield fumbled in his shirt pocket, but his hand came out empty.

"Reckon I must have left my makin's behind," he said. "Can you spare one?"

"Certainly, help yourself," Lee invited, extending the case.

Hatfield took one of the precisely rolled cigarettes and lighted it. He smoked slowly and his brain tablet was only half consumed when Lee snuffed out his butt. The engineer drew out his watch, glanced at it and shook his head.

"Looks like Radcliff went home," he remarked. "Well, I'll look in at the First Chance next door and if he isn't there, I'll be riding back to the camp. Work to do. Thanks for the drink."

With a nod, he left the saloon. Through the blue haze of his cigarette smoke, Hatfield watched him pass through the swinging doors. Then, very carefully, he snuffed out the cigarette.

However, he did not throw away the butt. He laid it on the table and from the twisted bit of paper in the buttoned pocket he took another butt, the one he had picked up the night he barely missed death under the cascading steel rails. His brows drew together as he compared the two.

They were both machine rolled cigarettes, tailor mades the cowhands called them, not often met with in a section where men roll their own. And the brands were the same!

Hatfield carefully stowed both butts in the paper and buttoned them in his pocket.

"Not much," he mused. "You can't hang a man for smoking a particular brand of cigarettes, but it sure is a bit of a coincidence that the jigger who tried to kill me that night was smoking the same brand Alton Lee smokes."

He paid for his dinner and left the saloon.

Hatfield knew where Alton Lee kept his horse. His own sorrel was hitched just a little down the street from the stable. He strolled to where Goldy stood and took up a position from where he could see the door of the stable just a little beyond the mouth of an alley.

A very little time had passed when the wide door swung open and a man rode out and turned up the alley. Hatfield could not see his face, but he was convinced it was Lee. He waited a minute or two, then forked Goldy and rode along a street that paralleled the alley. He knew that if Lee was headed for the railroad camp he would follow the Coronado Trail for a couple of miles and then turn west across the prairie.

Hatfield reached the trail and turned north. A little later, topping a rise a quarter of a mile ahead, he spotted his quarry. Lee was riding at a moderate pace and apparently gave no thought to the possibility of being followed, for as Hatfield drifted along behind him in the shadow, he never once turned his head.

A mile flowed under Goldy's irons, and a second. Hatfield closed the distance a little. The moon was still behind the hills, but by the reflected light he could make out the blurred form of the horseman ahead. Any minute now he should turn left from the trail.

However, he didn't turn left. He turned right, following a track that wound into the hills by way of a canyon. Hatfield quickened Goldy's pace and quickly reached the spot where Lee turned off. The canyon was shadowy but the moonlight was growing stronger. Hatfield hesitated an instant then turned into the canyon. Only a few hundred yards distant it curved sharply. Lee was nowhere in sight. Hatfield sent Goldy forward, slowing as he neared the curve. No telling what might be waiting for him beyond the jut of rock. He took a chance and nosed the sorrel ahead.

The trail straightened out and again he caught sight of Lee, now only a few hundred yards ahead. At least Hatfield supposed it was Lee. He had not yet gotten a glimpse of his face. Keeping in the shadow of the brush that flanked the trail he followed. Fortunately the track was of soft earth and comparatively free of stones.

Goldy's irons made only a whisper of sound on its surface. Hatfield could not hear the hoof beats of Lee's horse, so it was logical to believe that his quarry could not hear Goldy's.

"But if he turns around all of a sudden while we're passing an open space, he can't hardly miss spotting us," he told the sorrel. "And for Pete's sake, don't take a notion to sing a song or do some extra loud snorting."

Lee did not turn in his saddle. He rode on, eyes to the front, at a leisurely pace. He evidently knew exactly where he was going and, it seemed, had no reason to believe anybody might be tailing him.

They covered a mile or more. Then Lee abruptly swerved his mount to the left and vanished. Hatfield knew he must have entered a side canyon or a cleft in the rocky wall. Again he had to undergo the nerve wracking business of riding ahead without knowing whether the man he trailed was holed up waiting for him.

Matters weren't any better when he reached a cleft in the canyon wall. It was narrow and the track ran between stands of tall brush. Here very little moonlight penetrated and he couldn't see fifty feet in front of him.

"But we've gone this far and we might as

well keep on going," he told the sorrel. He rode very slowly, pausing from time to time to look and listen. The quarry couldn't turn off, for the walls beyond the bristle of growth were sheer; as long as prevailing conditions continued, there was no chance of him giving his pursuer the slip.

For perhaps half a mile the trail followed the winding crack, with only the almost opaque gloom always ahead. Then suddenly Hatfield saw a gleam of light. The brush was thinning a bit and a moment later it ended at a small clearing. The light he now saw came from the dusty window of a weatherbeaten but stoutly built cabin that sat in the middle of the clearing. It had doubtless once been the home of a prospector or trapper. There were many such scattered through the hills.

Hatfield pulled to a halt and sat eyeing the dark bulk of the building. He could see a shadow passing the window now and then. Presently he heard a sound of hammering. He hesitated a moment, then dismounted and forced Goldy into the brush. Then he slipped back to the outer fringe and again studied the lighted building.

He was itching for a glimpse of the interior of the cabin. Should he risk sneaking across the clearing and peering through the window? Or should he wait till Lee finished whatever he was doing and departed? The latter course appeared decidedly the more sensible. The moon was high in the sky now and flooding the clearing with silvery light. To try and cross the open space under such circumstances would be an act of lunacy. Lee, if it was Lee, would doubtless not take kindly to spying on his activities. And the fact that his saddled and bridled horse stood in front of the cabin door seemed to indicate that his stay would not be lengthy.

The only drawback in the latter plan was that he couldn't very well examine the cabin and keep trailing Lee at the same time. However, he felt that he was more likely to discover something of interest inside the building. When he left the cabin, Lee would probably head straight for the railroad camp.

"That is unless he comes out packing something," the Ranger muttered. "In that case, I figure I'd better keep the hellion in sight."

The wait was tediously long. Hatfield had about decided to risk a peek through the window when the occupant of the cabin came out and mounted his horse. He wasn't carrying anything.

Crouched in the growth Hatfield watched him ride past and vanish down the brush flanked trail. He tried hard to get a glimpse of his face, but it was in the shadow of a low-drawn hat brim and little more than a formless blur.

Hatfield waited till the whisper of hoof beats had ceased to be audible. Then he led Goldy from the growth and to the cabin, leaving him with trailing reins just outside the door. He cautiously entered the building, listened a moment and struck a match. There was a bracket lamp on the wall and he touched the flame to the wick. It flared up and revealed a single square room with a fireplace in one end and a bunk built against one wall.

It also revealed a miscellany of objects. There was a workbench built of rough planks, on which were scattered a number of wood-working tools. Over to one side was a box of dynamite, the lid laid back to show a row of the greasy cylinders. There were a few cooking utensils, and some staple provisions on a shelf; signs of considerable occupancy.

All this Hatfield noted in one swift, all-embracing glance. Then he examined the planes, chisels, saws and hammers. They were excellent tools and showed signs of use. The floor was littered with shavings and bits of wood. He picked up a fragment and gave it a careful once-over. It was burr oak.

"Hit on the jigger's workshop, it would seem," he muttered. "Reckon it was here he loaded up those ties with dynamite. This is getting interesting. And there's a big coil of fuse, too. He didn't employ fuse in those infernal machines he rigged up inside the crossties, but he must have when he blew that hole in the reservoir. From the supply he's got on hand, looks like he has other ideas for it. Well, I've a hunch what that will be."

His eyes roved about and he spotted a rifle hanging from pegs driven into the logs. He took it down and examined it curiously. It was a beautiful weapon, a short-barreled thirty-thirty repeater, and fully loaded.

It was Goldy's warning snort that saved him. Hatfield knew that suddenly explosive blow meant somebody was approaching. He was going sideways and down when the shotgun cut loose with a double report that was like to the thunderclap of doom.

The window flew to fragments. Buckshot screeched through the air and spatted against the far wall.

194

Deafened by the terrific crash, half blinded by the blaze of the discharge, Hatfield flung the rifle to his shoulder and sent a stream of lead hissing through the window as fast as he could work the magazine lever. He hurled the empty thirty-thirty at the bracket lamp, smashing out the light. Then, a gun in each hand, he glided through the darkness to the door, which stood open a crack. His ears stopped ringing and he heard a faint whisper of fast hoofs fading down the canyon. With a muttered oath he forked Goldy and set out in pursuit.

"If the hellion thinks he can outrun you, feller, he's got another thing coming," he grimly told the sorrel. "Sift sand! Here's where we get the lowdown on that infernal drygulcher!"

Goldy responded, lengthening his stride. He flashed between the growth flanking the trail, and in another instant was flying through the air.

Only the fact that he was flung into the brush saved Hatfield from a broken neck. As it was, he got plenty of bruises and scratches. All the breath was knocked from his body and he was half stunned by a stout branch that came in contact with his skull. It was minutes before he could stagger to his feet, gasping and panting.

His first thought was for his horse. He was intensely relieved when he saw Goldy on all fours; and if snorts could swear, Goldy was undoubtedly swearing.

A quick examination assured Hatfield that aside from skinned knees and a patch of hide knocked off one shoulder, Goldy had suffered no serious injury. Then he limped back up the trail in search of what had caused the sorrel to take that astounding header. There was little doubt in his mind as to what he would find.

A moment later he did find it — a rope stretched across the trail at just the right height to trip a speeding horse.

Hatfield leaned against a convenient tree trunk, rolled a cigarette and smoked until his nerves had steadied.

"Never misses a bet," he muttered. "Arranged his get-away if something should slip. Laid a nice little trap for me, and I walked into it like a dumb yearling. He knew all the time I was trailing him. That's why he mentioned, there in the saloon, that he was riding back to the railroad camp right away. Figured I'd swallow the bait and amble after him just as I did. After he left the cabin he rode down the trail a little ways and waited till I'd be absorbed in my snooping. Then he slipped back and threw down on me with his scattergun. And if it hadn't been for Goldy letting off that blow when he did, the sidewinder would have spattered me all over the walls.

"And the most aggravating part of the whole business is that he got away with it," he added morosely. "Not a way in the world for me to tie him up with anything. I never did get a look at his face. He took good care that I didn't, and I didn't catch on. All I could say is that I trailed some jigger out of town and that somebody took a shot at me. Accuse Lee of being the jigger? I'd just make a laughing stock of myself. Might as well admit the truth, he's outsmarted me at every turn. Well, things can't go on this way forever. Sooner or later it'll be showdown, and curtains for one of us, and I'm darned if I'd want to bet on which one it will be!"

Sore in every joint and muscle and with his bruised head throbbing unpleasantly, he returned to his horse and, thoroughly disgusted with things in general, including himself, headed for the lumber camp.

As to what he had found in the cabin he gave little thought. Nothing there that could be used as evidence against Lee or anybody else and he felt sure the place would never be used again. What had looked like a promising lead had fizzled out.

"Well, anyhow it's Sunday and I can sleep late," he told Goldy. "I figure I need it."

CHAPTER 17

Hatfield did sleep late, not awakening till mid-morning. Aside from a few scratches and bruises and a sore head he felt pretty good. After a leisurely breakfast he talked a while with Clark Wallace, discussing various phases of the logging business. Then he got the rig on Goldy.

"I'm going for a bit of a ride," he told the lumberman. "Don't expect to be gone long. Stick around till I get back. May have something important for you."

"Okay," Wallace agreed, "I'll be around. Got plenty of work to do in the office."

It was not long after noon when he sighted a big white ranchhouse advantageously set in a grove. He knew it must be Bull Radcliff's Lazy B. There was a man sitting on the wide veranda and as he drew near he recognized Radcliff himself.

Hatfield rode up to the veranda, dropped the split reins to the ground and dismounted. With a nod to Radcliff, who looked puzzled and resentful, he strolled up the steps and surveyed the ranch owner for a moment.

"Mind if I sit down?" he asked.

"Suit yourself," Radcliff grunted and still looked unpleasant. But his expression gradually changed to one of defiance as Hatfield's steady gaze never left his face.

"And I suppose you figured me for a darned murderer, just like the rest of them," he growled.

Hatfield shook his head, fished out the makin's and rolled a cigarette.

"Nope," he said, "I figure you in the same class as a thickheaded old shorthorn bull butting a barbed wire fence and bellerin' because the spikes prick him. And by your cussed contrariness and mulishness and 'I-know-what's-best-for-everybody' attitude you've succeeded in getting yourself on a very hot spot. It's going to take considerable maneuvering to get you off. Shut up, now, and wait till I've finished!"

Radcliff, who had opened his mouth to reply, gulped, making a sound like a pig with a rattlesnake's tail caught in its throat.

"Yes, you're on a spot," Hatfield repeated. "Radcliff, do you realize that there's enough circumstantial evidence against you to warrant your arrest on a murder charge? And with the community in its present temper a conviction would very likely result."

The color had drained from Radcliff's face as Hatfield spoke. He raised a trembling hand to wipe his suddenly damp forehead.

"I'm — I'm afraid you could be right," he answered in a quivering voice.

"And if I'd formed just a little different estimate of you, I'd be taking you back to town with me," Hatfield added. He held his Ranger star for Radcliff to see as he spoke.

Radcliff stared at the symbol of law and order, his eyes widening. He wet his dry lips with the tip of his tongue. But when he looked up his eyes met the Ranger's squarely.

"Hatfield," he said thickly, "I ain't guilty."

"If you were, I wouldn't be sitting here talking with you," Hatfield replied. "However, a lot of folks believe you are, and that has to be considered. It's time for you to take inventory and realize your actions are responsible for what you're up against. You've accused Clark Wallace of flimflamming you in a deal. He didn't. You've accused your friends of double-crossing you. They didn't. You've blamed everybody for your troubles except the one person who is to blame — yourself."

"I — I guess maybe you're right," Radcliff admitted.

"I am right," Hatfield said. "Now we've got to figure a way to undo the damage. I'm going to ask you a few questions, and I want straight answers. Guess you know about as much concerning Alton Lee's business as anybody hereabouts, don't you?"

"Why — I guess I do," Radcliff hesitated.

"Okay. Is it true that if Lee completes his project in time to beat the C & P to Alpine Pass he'll get a big bonus in T & W stock?"

"That's right," Radcliff replied.

"And does he own considerable T & W stock already?"

"Understand he does," said Radcliff. "I know he's bought up quite a few loose blocks. The stock went down a while back, you know."

"And," pursued Hatfield, "do you think that with his bonus he'd own enough to control the T & W system?"

"I couldn't say as to that," answered Radcliff, "but I've a notion he wouldn't need overly much more to do so. Why are you asking all this about Lee?"

"There is a Ranger axiom," Hatfield replied. "It says, 'find the motive.'"

Radcliff blinked. "You mean to say you think Lee might be responsible for what's been going on?" he asked incredulously.

"He is," Hatfield replied tersely.

"Then why don't you arrest him?"

Hatfield smiled for the first time during the interview. "Isn't so simple as that," he replied. "Knowing something and proving it are two different matters. So far I haven't enough proof to convict Lee of anything, and if such a charge were brought against him, he'd end up hanging you higher than Haman. He's maneuvered you into a position where you'd make a nice little scapegoat for him. He's led you to make statements, before witnesses, that would be damning if brought up in court. He wouldn't have a bit of trouble showing that he was innocent and had been taken in by you who, motivated by a desire for revenge, did the things that caused men to die."

Radcliff's face had whitened as Hatfield spoke. He evidently recalled some of the things he had said and the threats he had made.

"Yes, he'd hang you higher than Haman," Hatfield repeated, adding with another smile, "but maybe we can turn the tables on him and cause him to end up as Haman did, who played a somewhat similar role a few thousand years back."

"Who the devil's Haman?" Radcliff asked. "I never heard of him."

"You'll find him in the Bible," Hatfield replied. "He was a conniver who built a gallows fifty cubits high on which to hang an innocent man, a right jigger named Mordecai, but Queen Esther outsmarted the conniver and the king had Haman hanged on the gallows he built for Mordecai."

Radcliff grinned wanly. "Reckon I know about how Mordecai felt," he said. "But what the devil's to be done?"

"Several things," Hatfield answered. "First off, we're going to take a little ride — up to Clark Wallace's lumber camp."

Radcliff looked startled, but didn't offer any objection.

"Is your daughter Helen home?" Hatfield asked.

"Why, I guess she is," Radcliff admitted. "Must be in back somewhere."

"Reckon she'd better ride with us," Hatfield said.

"Ride with us! Why in blazes —"

Hatfield interrupted, "It's like this, Helen and Clark want to get married, and they'll feel a lot better if you come along now and tell Clark it's okay with you and that you'll be proud to have such a fine, upstanding, capable son-in-law."

Radcliff gulped, and goggled. "Why — why — why that young whippersnapper!" he sputtered.

Hatfield chuckled. "I wonder just what Helen's mother's dad called you when you came courting her?" he remarked.

Radcliff tried to look indignant. Then he grinned, and suddenly his bad-tempered old face looked strangely youthful.

"Among other things, I rec'lect the old pelican threatened to take a shotgun to me," he admitted.

"But he didn't, and you'll not take one to Wallace," Hatfield said cheerfully. "Okay, call Helen and get your horses and we'll ride."

Radcliff threw out his hands in despair. "I've a notion you always get your way with everybody, sooner or later. All right, I been figuring for quite a while this whole darn business would drive me loco. Reckon it has." He stood up, shaking his head as in disbelief that it really could have happened to him.

"And I reckon I can depend on you to keep your mouth shut," Hatfield remarked significantly as he replaced the Ranger star in its secret pocket.

"You can," Radcliff replied and entered the house.

Astounded, flabbergasted, utterly thunderstruck — all were too mild to describe Clark Wallace's condition when Hatfield with Helen and Bull Radcliff rode up to the lumber camp. However, he managed to recover enough to dazedly shake hands with his future father-in-law.

Later, Hatfield and Radcliff walked up the flume to the reservoir wall.

"And that is what pretty well convinced me that neither you nor Chuck Hooley was responsible for the goings-on hereabouts," Hatfield said, pointing to the jagged hole in the cliff. "I was certain neither of you had the necessary knowledge of petrology to spot that fault in the rock and understood what it meant."

"Huh!" snorted Radcliff. "I don't even know what the word means, and Chuck wouldn't know it if he met it in the middle of the road."

"So I gathered," Hatfield nodded. "That's where Lee tipped his hand, too, although at first I could hardly believe it. For quite a while I kept thinking about Hooley, wondering if I had made a mistake in my estimate of him, but I finally decided I hadn't. That left Lee as the only person I'd contacted who was capable of doing the chore. Of course all I had was suspicion, but subsequent events strengthened my conviction that Lee was my man. Now I know he is, but I still haven't a bit of proof against him; nothing that would stand up in court. It's up to me to get the proof, and here's where you come into the picture. I want you to keep close tabs on Lee and report anything that appears out of the ordinary. We'll keep things secret and warn Helen and Wallace to do likewise. There'll be no reason for him to suspect that we've gotten together."

"Right," agreed Radcliff, "and I'll set Chuck Hooley to watching him, too. Hooley's a master tracker; I believe he's part Indian. He'll never let Lee out of his sight and Lee will never know he's being trailed. Chuck is ornery as a tarantula, but he knows how to keep his mouth shut and he's faithful to me. I saved his worthless life for him once and he's never forgotten it."

"Sounds good," admitted Hatfield, "but don't forget, if Lee catches on, your lives won't be worth a busted cartridge. He's smart and utterly ruthless. He's playing for big stakes and he's out to win. I imagine he's getting pretty desperate about now, though, and that may cause him to make a reckless move and tip his hand. Would be a good idea, if you can work it, and I don't see any reason that you can't, to slow up production a bit. Have your sawmill break down, or some of your men quit or something like that. You should be able to do it without exciting suspicion."

"I'll work it," Radcliff promised. His face twisted with vindictive anger. "I'm out to get that sidewinder. I can see now how he's been egging me on to do and say things against my better judgment. As you said a while back, I've been a plumb darn fool, but I don't intend to keep on being one.

"Do you figure Lee knows you're a Ranger?" he added curiously.

"I think he knows everything there is to know about me," Hatfield replied grimly. "I'm of the opinion that he recognized me the first time he saw me, figured I was here to investigate and decided I'd best be gotten out of the way in a hurry. The Rangers have a habit of nosing things out, you know. He very nearly succeeded the first time, and he wasn't a bit discouraged when he failed in his attempt."

"Nerve enough to kill a Ranger!" Radcliff marvelled.

"Killing a Ranger is no different from killing anybody else, if you don't get caught at it," Hatfield pointed out. "If he'd succeeded in any of the tries he made for me, he never would have gotten caught; and before somebody else was sent here and got the lowdown on things the chances are he'd have put over one of his schemes and had easy going from there on. He's a cold proposition with plenty of savvy."

"Smart as a treeful of owls and dangerous as a nest of rattlers," agreed Radcliff. "Well, I guess I'd better pick up Helen and head back to the ranch. Don't worry, you can depend on me for everything. And, Hatfield, much obliged for making an ornery old maverick finally see things in the right way."

After Radcliff and Helen departed, Clark Wallace turned to Hatfield.

"Jim," he said, "how in blazes did you do it?"

CHAPTER 18

Several uneventful days passed. Hatfield heard nothing from Radcliff.

But he did hear there had been a bad accident at Radcliff's sawmill. The night watchman had let the water get low in the boiler and burned the crown sheet. It would take a couple of days, perhaps more, to repair the damage and get the mill back into production.

"And Senor Lee must be getting frantic," he mused. "If he's ever going to pull something, he should pull it soon."

Another day passed and Hatfield grew acutely uneasy. He had an unpleasant premonition that disaster was due to strike.

With the passage of still a second day he still heard nothing from Radcliff, and was not particularly surprised. Despite Radcliff's faith in Chuck Hooley as a tracker, Hatfield had good reason to believe that tailing Alton Lee, if Lee didn't want to be tailed, would be considerable of a chore for Hooley or anybody else. Toward nightfall he resolved to ride to town on the chance that he might pick up some stray bit of information. Shortly after dark he got the rig on Goldy and started out.

At the edge of the clearing he paused to gaze up at the cliff rim shimmering against the sky, and to listen to the steady clank of the rams. Then he rode on and turned into the Coronado Trail. The sky was brilliant with stars that cast a ghostly light over the winding gray ribbon.

Hatfield rode slowly, deep with thought. The night was deathly still and the gray silence affected his nerves, already tightly strung. Each clump of brush seemed to waver with a stealthy menace and standing beside the road were things that he knew to be trees but which his imagination endowed with sinister movement, their crooked branches like to reaching arms and clutching hands. Goldy seemed to be affected, too, for he snorted nervously and tossed his head from time to time. Hatfield swore at himself for letting his imagination run riot, but an eerie feeling persisted that he was riding toward trouble. So much so that he was more than usually alert.

He had covered perhaps half the distance to town and had just topped a rise when in the clear, still evening air there sounded the sharp, hard note of a single gunshot.

Instinctively he jerked Goldy to a halt and sat listening, his tall form outlined against the starry sky. The sound was not repeated and he heard nothing more.

Ahead the trail writhed downward between stands of brush to vanish in the deep shadows at the bottom of the sag. It was from that dark pool of shadow several hundred yards distant that the ominous sound had come.

Hatfield hesitated. He didn't like the looks of that still gloom at the base of the slope, but he felt called upon to investigate without delay. Getting a grip on himself, he sent Goldy slowly down the sag, every nerve and sense strung to hair-trigger alertness.

Still the silence persisted. He reached the bottom of the slope and slowed the sorrel still more. Now that he was closer, the shadows ahead appeared less opaque and a moment later he made out something standing beside the trail. A few more slow paces and he saw it was a saddled and bridled horse that stood motionless, split reins hanging. And in the center of the trail lay what he quickly identified as the body of a man.

With an exclamation, Hatfield dismounted and approached the body. He had almost reached it, when he heard a slight rustling in the growth to his left, as if somebody had shifted position. He whirled sideways to face the black wall of brush. The crash of a shot shattered the silence. The bullet plowed a stinging furrow along his ribs and the shock of the blow knocked him back, reeling. He tripped over something and fell heavily in the deeper shadow beside the trail. Rolling over he whipped out his guns and sprayed the brush with slugs, weaving the muzzles back and forth. Thumbs on the cocked hammers he held his fire and listened. He thought he heard a crackling in the bush a little farther up the trail and sent two bullets in the direction of the sound. He ejected the spent shells from his guns and replaced them with fresh cartridges. Then he lay rigid, debating on what to do.

To cross the open track would be sheer madness. For all he knew the drygulcher was holed up waiting, just as he had waited for him to appear and investigate the dead man lying in the dust, doubtless having spotted him sitting his horse on the crest of the rise.

A little distance ahead the growth interlaced over the trail and there the gloom was intense. He got cautiously to his hands and knees and, careful not to make the slightest sound, crawled slowly along in the shadow. When he reached the black dark under the spreading branches he rose to his feet and slipped across the track to the growth on the far side. Slowly, carefully, he worked north toward where he had heard the sound, pausing often to peer and listen. With meticulous care he covered the ground for a wide area, finally becoming convinced that the killer had really departed. Giving up the hunt he made his way back to the trail, knelt beside the body, which lay face downward, and turned it over. There was little doubt in his mind as to who it was.

He was right. It was Chuck Hooley and he had been shot through the side of the head.

"Poor devil never knew what hit him," Hatfield muttered. "Well, he may have been an excellent tracker, but he wasn't good enough to go up against that snake-blooded hellion. Lee must have caught on, led him along and after passing through that patch of dense shadow, where Hooley couldn't see him, holed up and waited for him to show. Not a nerve in his body! And thinks no more of killing a man than he would of swatting a fly. I've been up against some hard characters in my time, but nothing to equal him. Well, maybe things will change after a while, but I've a notion time is running out."

He picked up Hooley's body, wincing from the pain of his bullet-burned ribs, and draped it across the saddle of the patiently waiting horse, securing it in place with his tie rope. Then he mounted Goldy and leading Hooley's horse with its grisly burden, continued on to town and the sheriff's office.

Even the hardened old peace officer was a bit shaken when Hatfield carried what was left of Hooley into his office and deposited it on a couch.

"My God! When is it ever going to end!" he exclaimed.

"I don't know," Hatfield replied soberly. "He seems to have an uncanny ability to sense everything that's going on and to be always one jump ahead."

"This is terrible," muttered McGregor, "and, Jim, it sort of puts you on a spot. It's known there was bad blood between you and Hooley. Folks may do some thinking. I've a notion it wouldn't be a bad idea for you to pin your Ranger star on your shirt."

"I've a feeling you might be right," Hatfield agreed. "Not much gained in covering up any longer. I'm pretty well convinced that Lee knows I'm a Ranger and doesn't give a darn. Well, we'll see. Guess you'd better send word to Radcliff and let him come and get Hooley's body. He'll understand what happened. I'm going over to the Greasy Sack and get a drink. Then I'll head back for the camp. No sense in hanging around here. If anything else busts loose, I've a notion it will be up there."

The following day, Hatfield's pertubation had increased until he felt he couldn't take much more. Lee might be frantic over the delay of his project, but Hatfield had to admit that he was becoming a bit frantic, too. Who would be the next to die, if he wasn't able to drop a loop on the sidewinder without delay? Very probably Bull Radcliff. Lee would know that Hooley hadn't been acting on his own initiative and would quickly decide that Radcliff had been the moving force behind the logging foreman. Perhaps Lee's need for Radcliff to get out the timber for him might save the rancher for a while, but eventually, Hatfield was convinced, Radcliff's number would be up.

He tried to put himself in Lee's place and figure just what he would do under the circumstances. The results were not satisfactory.

But out of his ponderings came a hunch. He had written off the cabin in the canyon the night he came near to getting blown to bits. Now gradually he began to wonder if his judgment had been sound. The place was Lee's workshop, and doubtless his base of supplies. It wasn't logical to think he'd return to the place to which he had been tracked, but could Lee be depended upon to do the logical thing. It was not beyond the realm of possibility that he had deduced just what would be Hatfield's estimate of the situation. His crafty mind might well reason along just such lines and arrive at the conclusion that Hatfield would give the cabin no more thought. In which event he would decide it would be safe to return if it was to the advantage of his plans to do so.

"And it would be like the nervy sidewinder to do just that," Hatfield mused. "He's not the ordinary brush-popping brand of owlhoot, and so far he's managed to keep one jump ahead of me. I've tried to keep up with him by doing what appeared to be the sensible and reasonable thing to do. Hasn't worked so well. I'll play a hunch and do what I'm not supposed to do. Better than just sitting around waiting for something to pop."

His mind made up, he saddled Goldy and rode south till he reached the track that led to the cabin. Taking no chances, he approached the clearing with caution, leaving Goldy ensconced in the brush some distance down the trail and covering the remaining distance on foot.

The clearing was deserted, the cabin unlighted. Hatfield found a suitable spot in the growth, holed up and waited. The moon had not yet risen, but the sky was brilliant with stars and by their wan light he could make out objects.

The hours passed slowly and tediously, and nothing happened. Nothing moved on the trail, no sound, save the occasional call of some night bird broke the silence. Finally, when the east was graying, he gave up in disgust and rode back to the logging camp in a very bad frame of mind.

But the hunch persisted, and an hour after nightfall found Hatfield again holed up in the brush beside the clearing.

It lacked a couple of hours to midnight when he heard the beat of a horse's hoofs on the trail and steadily drawing nearer. The night was very dark and when a man rode into the clearing, his form was but a misty blur. He was little more than a moving shadow when he dismounted in front of the cabin.

A moment later a light flared up inside the building. Hatfield watched it and tried to decide what to do. He could slip across to the cabin in the darkness, get the drop on Lee and confront him.

Confront him with what? There was no law against a man being in a deserted cabin that Hatfield ever heard tell of. Nor against making a workshop of one, for that matter. Might appear strange that he should be there, but trust Lee to have a plausible explanation all ready.

Accuse him of cutting loose the shotgun blast that came so near to killing him? Again, where was his proof? He'd have to admit he didn't see Lee's face. Lee could swear he hadn't been near the cabin for a week, and that Hatfield had merely tangled with some unauthorized prowler. No, he still had nothing against Lee that would stand up. The only thing was to await developments.

Lee didn't remain long in the cabin. The light went out and a moment later Hatfield saw him ride across the clearing and vanish into the blackness of the brush flanked trail. Hatfield waited a brief period, then hurried to where he had left Goldy and rode cautiously in the engineer's wake. He knew he was taking a chance, the darkness being what it was, but felt he had to risk it.

The ride down the canyon was not pleasant. If the canny Lee should suspect that he might have been spied on and was taking precautions against being trailed, the results would very likely be disastrous for Hatfield. He breathed deep relief when he reached the canyon mouth and the Coronado Trail lay before him, shimmering in the pale light of the gibbous moon just peeping over the hill crests.

Taking care to keep in the shadow, Hatfield rode out upon the trail. Immediately he sighted his quarry, riding nearly half a mile ahead. He followed, careful to keep in the shadow.

And then Lee abruptly turned to the left and rode across the open rangeland, heading north by west, toward the site of the T & W railroad camp.

Hatfield pulled up with a disgusted oath. To all appearances, Lee was headed for the camp. And anyhow there was no following him across the moon drenched prairie that afforded not a spot of cover. He morosely watched Lee grow small in the distance, then turned and rode back to the logging camp. Another promising lead had fizzled.

But he hadn't been at the camp an hour before his former uneasiness returned. The feeling that something was going to happen grew stronger, until it was like to an urgent voice calling. He told himself it was all nonsense, excitement caused by the strain he was under. But, cold reason to the contrary, the feeling persisted to such an extent that sleep was impossible. He left the camp office in which he was sitting and walked out into the night. For long minutes he stood gazing at the crest of the grim cliffs that walled in the natural reservoir. They loomed black and forbidding against the sky, reflected moonlight edging the towering rim with ghostly fire.

That palely shimmering rim drew him like a lodestone. And up there, where the cracked and broken north wall hung over the opening from which the spring of vital earth gushed forth was the weak link in the chain that held the lumbering project together.

But, darn it, there was an alert guard stationed up there against any such threat to the all-important water supply. Then he recalled the vicious shrewdness of Alton Lee and began to get worried once more. What if Lee, as on the former occasion, had known or suspected he was being trailed tonight and had deliberately turned toward the railroad camp to throw him off guard. Hatfield had given up the chase. Perhaps Lee had figured that was just what he would do and after making sure he was no longer observed, had turned back to his objective, whatever that might be. And if he didn't have something definite in mind, why had he risked visiting the cabin again?

Hatfield gave up fighting the urge to have a look at the cliff tops. He got the rig on Goldy, cursing himself for an imaginative fool the while.

Once started, he wasted no time but circled swiftly through the timber till he came to the gentle north slope that led to the rim of the reservoir. Here he slowed up, listening for any sound, watching for any movement on the brush grown sag. Some distance below the cliff crests he dismounted and continued on foot, stealing stealthily through the growth, for unless he chose to announce himself, he must approach the rim with caution. Should he startle the guard stationed there, he might have to dodge lead.

Hatfield knew where the watchman had built a little leanto for protection against the wind. He made for the leanto, moving at a snail's pace. He reached the incline of brush and poles but saw nothing of the guard; perhaps he was patrolling the rim. He waited several moments, then carefully edged around to the front of the leanto. The sky had become slightly overcast with filmy clouds but enough moonlight filtered through to show something lying in front of the leanto, something that Hatfield quickly recognized as the body of a man, doubtless the guard. It looked like the fellow was asleep.

He moved a little closer. It was the guard, all right, lying half on his side. Hatfield reached down and tapped his shoulder gently. He did not move. Hatfield tapped a little harder; but still the man lay without sound or motion. Abruptly very much concerned, Hatfield slid his hand up over the fellow's face and encountered an unpleasant stickiness, and the man's features had an ominous rigidity. Hatfield peered closer, and stifled an exclamation.

The guard was dead, his face visored by partially congealed blood. A moment's examination revealed a ghastly wound just above his left temple. He had been struck a crushing blow with something hard and heavy.

Hatfield straightened up, glancing about. There was nobody in sight, but somebody had been here just a few minutes before, and had committed murder.

The lip of the curving cliff was less than a hundred yards distant. Directly below the rim was the cracked and shattered fault above where the spring gushed from the opening in the reservoir wall. Hatfield moved toward the rim, swiftly but silently. He had covered half the distance when he heard a scraping, scratching sound ahead. He quickened his pace and was less than a dozen feet distant when something loomed above the rocky lip. He bounded forward as a man levered himself over the rim, and surged erect. The moonlight fell full on his face. It was Alton Lee!

Hatfield saw Lee's right arm shoot out. He made a frantic grab for Lee's wrist, missed, but managed to knock his hand up as the deadly double-barrelled derringer boomed its twin reports. The blaze of flame from the stubby barrels singed his face and blinded him. His hat was whisked from his head by the heavy slugs; his ears rang to the crash.

There was no time to go for his guns. Lee's hand had already streaked across his chest to his armpit, where he packed a shoulder gun. This time Hatfield got his wrist before he could pull trigger. At the same instant, Lee's other hand closed on the Ranger's throat with a throttling grip. And his fingers seemed made of steel springs.

Hatfield grabbed the hand and forced it back far enough to save his larynx from being crushed, but he could not break Lee's terrible hold. Nor could he loosen his grasp on the other's wrist. If he did so he would get the contents of that shoulder gun dead center.

Back and forth they wrestled, in grim silence save for the hissing of their breath and the pound of their boots on the crumbling edge of the cliff with seventy feet of nothing beneath. Lee had swung Hatfield around till his back was to the gulf and was fighting to force him over the lip. And his strength was the strength of a madman. He did get one foot over but Hatfield surged forward with every ounce of his strength and recovered in the nick of time.

But that awful grip was choking the breath in his throat. His lungs were bursting. Red flashes stormed before his eyes. And Lee's gun hand was coming around inch by steady inch. Just a little more and he would have the muzzle in line with Hatfield's breast. His eyes flashed with triumph. Another inch and he would pull trigger.

In desperation Hatfield made one last frantic gamble. Not knowing how near he was to the cliff edge, he hurled himself backward and down. He fully expected to feel himself hurtling through the air to the rocky floor nigh a hundred feet below. Instead his back struck the ground with stunning force. At the same instant he shot one foot upward and jerked on Lee's wrists with all his might.

As Lee's body rose in the air, Hatfield's foot, with his leg rigid as a steel bar, caught the engineer squarely in the middle. Hatfield thrust upward and let go Lee's wrists.

Lee uttered his first sound, a wild, despairing cry as he cleared the cliff's edge and shot downward. Dimly, through a haze of pain and near exhaustion, Hatfield heard the thud of his broken body on the rocks below.

For a moment Hatfield lay retching and gasping, trembling in every limb. Then he got drunkenly to his knees, crawled to the rim and peered downward.

A rope dangled down the jagged wall, and a score of feet below a hissing, sputtering flower of fire was crawling slowly up the cliff. Lee had planted a dynamite charge in the weakened wall above the spring. At any instant it would explode and hermetically seal the source of the precious water forever.

Hatfield took a deep breath, gripped the rope and went down it hand over hand. He reached a point where he could reach out and grasp the burning fuse, twined the rope around his leg and tried to fumble his knife from his pocket.

He couldn't do it! Strain as he would, he could not reach around far enough with his free hand. If he let go the shortening fuse, he would not be able to grasp it again. And the fire was now but inches from the cap that would explode the charge and hurl him to destruction.

Contorting his body into almost a circle, he got the fuse between his teeth and chewed frantically. The tough fibres resisted stubbornly, then gave. A gush of sparks seared the roof of his mouth; the fire was fairly lapping the cap!

There was but one thing to do. He took the frightful chance of jerking the cap free from the charge. A hard, steady pull brought no results. Hatfield set his teeth, tensed for the roar of the explosion he would never hear, and put forth his strength. He felt the cap loosen, grip, loosen again. One more desperate try! The cap tore free. He hurled the sputtering fuse far out through the air, saw it trail its glittering sparks downward. It struck the ground and for an instant the bluish glare showed the dead face of Alton Lee who lay on the rocky floor, his arms flung wide. Then the cap exploded with a sharp crack and the light snuffed out. Hatfield turned and began the terrible climb up the cliff.

Every mottling, crack and seam of that jagged wall was ever after stamped indelibly on his memory. The distance seemed a thousand feet instead of a mere twenty. The rope swayed and jerked, seemed to slip. He wondered dully how securely Lee had fastened it. Surely he must have made certain it was firm before descending to plant the charge. Then the dangling cord slipped again. Firm enough for his lighter weight, perhaps, but . . .

And then he was over the lip, the jagged edge shredding the flesh of his breast. His muscles were turning to water. He felt himself sliding back into the gulf. One last supreme effort, with death the forfeit for failure! He found himself crawling across the rimrock. With a groan he collapsed in a coma of complete exhaustion.

When he finally recovered consciousness

he saw from the moon that he must have been insensible for quite two hours. He was drenched with dew and shivering all over. He raised his head and was instantly taken with a violent sickness, the result of intense over-exertion, and very nearly passed out a second time. For several minutes he lay still, then tried it again. This time the crawling nausea wasn't so bad. He got stiffly to his feet, his teeth chattering with the cold, and lurched and stumbled down the trail to where he left his horse. After a couple of attempts he managed to mount the sorrel and give him his head. Goldy set out for home, his rider hunched forward till his face was buried in the horse's mane.

But before he reached the camp, Hatfield had recovered enough to sit straight in the saddle. He stabled Goldy, gave him as good a rubdown as he could under the circumstances and tumbled into bed. It was mid morning when he awakened to find Clark Wallace bending over him with an anxious face.

"Glad to see you open your eyes," Wallace said in relieved tones. "You looked like a dead man lying there. What in blazes happened?"

Hatfield painfully raised himself on one elbow and began to talk.

After the astounded lumberman had listened to the details of the night's grisly happenings, they brought the bodies of Lee and the murdered guard back to camp. Hatfield's eyes were regretful as he gazed down at Alton Lee's face.

"Gambled his life against a million, and lost," he said. "A man of great ambitions, high courage and outstanding brain power. He should have gone far. But some twist of his brilliant mind set him to riding a crooked trail, with the usual result. He played for high stakes and played his hand well, but not quite well enough. Made the little slips the owlhoot brand always makes. Like dropping a cigarette butt at the wrong place, and tieing an unusual knot in a rope. And if he'd thought to steal a few live oak crossties for his infernal machines instead of planting them in burr oaks, he wouldn't have left the corral gate wide open like he did."

He paused to roll a cigarette and glance toward his saddled and bridled horse.

"I'll stop in town and tell Sheriff McGregor to ride up and take charge of the body," he added. "Reckon you can get along comfortably with your lumber business now, and Bull Radcliff can hold his head up again. Say good-bye to Helen for me and tell her I said I'm sorry I can't stay for the wedding. Chances are Captain Bill will have another little vacation lined up for me by the time I get back to the Post. That's what he said this chore would be. I've a feeling he sort of missed his throw."

A little later Wallace watched him ride away, tall and graceful atop his great golden horse, the late sunlight etching his sternly handsome profile in flame, to where duty called and new adventure waited.

We hope you have enjoyed this Large Print book. Other Thorndike, Wheeler or Chivers Press Large Print books are available at your library or directly from the publishers.

For more information about current and upcoming titles, please call or write, without obligation, to:

Publisher
Thorndike Press
295 Kennedy Memorial Drive
Waterville, ME 04901
Tel. (800) 223-1244

Or visit our Web site at:
www.gale.com/thorndike
www.gale.com/wheeler

OR

Chivers Large Print
published by BBC Audiobooks Ltd
St James House, The Square
Lower Bristol Road
Bath BA2 3SB
England
Tel. +44(0) 800 136919
email: bbcaudiobooks@bbc.co.uk
www.bbcaudiobooks.co.uk

All our Large Print titles are designed for easy reading, and all our books are made to last.